THE SUCCUBUS

THE SUCCUBUS
A NOVEL BY VLADO ŽABOT

TRANSLATED BY RAWLEY GRAU AND NIKOLAI JEFFS

DALKEY ARCHIVE PRESS
CHAMPAIGN AND LONDON

Originally published in Slovenian as *Sukub* by Študentska založba, 2003
Copyright © 2003 by Vlado Žabot
Translation copyright © 2007 by Rawley Grau and Nikolai Jeffs
First edition, 2010
All rights reserved

Library of Congress Cataloging-in-Publication Data

Žabot, Vlado.
 [Sukub. English]
 The succubus / Vlado Zabot ; translated by Rawley Grau and Nikolai Jeffs. -- 1st ed.
   p. cm.
 Reissue of the translation published in Ljubljana by the Slovene Writers' Association,
2007.
 ISBN 978-1-56478-595-4 (pbk. : alk. paper)
 1. Succubi--Fiction. I. Grau, Rawley. II. Jeffs, Nikolai. III. Title.
 PG1919.36.A24S8513 2010
 891.8'435--dc22
                    2010011705

Partially funded by the University of Illinois at Urbana-Champaign, as well as by grants
from the National Endowment for the Arts, a federal agency, and the Illinois Arts Council,
a state agency

This work has been published with the financial support of the Trubar Foundation, located
at the Slovene Writers' Association, Ljubljana, Slovenia

The Slovenian Literature Series is made possible by support from the Slovenian Book Agency

www.dalkeyarchive.com

Cover: design and composition by Danielle Dutton, illustration by Nicholas Motte
Printed on permanent/durable acid-free paper and bound in the United States of America

For Eva and Mitja

1

This was hardly the first time Valent Kosmina had been unsettled by the thought that someone had pushed or seduced him—or that he had himself, perhaps out of clumsiness or carelessness, simply strayed—into a situation that would later be difficult to get out of. This idea, this fear, was in fact quite familiar to him, and naturally it unnerved him, but never to the degree that he couldn't shrug it off. A sensible person, after all, manages in one way or another to persuade himself that he is all right, that he is sufficiently in control of himself, and that life will therefore run its course, peacefully and properly, to its bitter end.

Nor was this the first time he had been tormented by insomnia. There had been periods, even back when he still had some job or another, when he didn't really know what to do with himself. Strange and useless thoughts would cross his mind. When he did sleep, his dreams were even stranger.

Meanwhile, despite all the empty apartments and derelict buildings, the city was peculiarly lively, always humming its low hum. Meanwhile, everyone—mostly old people, for whatever reason—seemed to be rushing off somewhere or other, overtaking one other, always hustling and bustling; and the streets, roads, and avenues were engulfed in a stifling haze. And, too, at times it seemed to him that there was something wrong with all those elderly people hurrying along the street, acting so energetic and youthful—perhaps, in reality, many of them no longer had anywhere to live . . . And above the crowded rooftops and domes, the bell towers and apartment blocks, isolated puffs of white steam, each far apart from the others, twisted lazily, continually into the sky. As he watched them through his living-room window on the fifteenth floor of his apartment building, he imagined that they came from slaughterhouses, though he'd never tried to confirm it. And looming above the more distant puffs, the ones just below the eastern horizon, there would usually appear, at the first morning light, a bigger, billowing, mountain-like cloud.

At times this cloud would seem cold and gray, sometimes savage, sometimes pale and indistinct, but at other times it was pleasantly warm and gentle, glowing softly at its edges. The shape of the cloud, too, was constantly changing. And, based on these variations in the cloud, Valent eventually (he didn't really know when or why, it just seemed to happen) found himself making predictions about what the day would bring, what he should avoid doing, and what, indeed, he would have to do in order to make everything turn out well and good.

Later, after he had been forced to retire, after his two sons had moved away to their own respective futures in their own respective apartment blocks, and after his wife, who had retired the year before, had succumbed to tranquilizers and television—when, in short, he no longer had any work problems or family matters to worry about—he thought he might finally have reached the point where he could get over those ridiculous ideas of his, which could really be quite unpleasant, about the old people rushing around on the street and then the prophetic cloud. But even then he wasn't able to get up the courage. He began to feel a suspicious stabbing pain in his heart. But there was no way he could tell anyone about any of this. Not even his wife. He would be too embarrassed. Humiliated, even. His look of noble, long-suffering self-confidence, which for some time now he had been obsessively cultivating (most especially with his pipe between his teeth)—this guise of his would be exposed as nothing but common duplicity and dissemblance.

Even now, in fact, he was quite proud of how convincingly he managed it, though naturally it required constant care, constant maintenance, so much so in fact that sometimes, when the opportunity presented itself, it made sense for him to turn off the street and make his way to the door of this or that law firm or notary office and jot down its office hours in his appointment book . . . Of course, people had always been mistrustful of him, had always been wary, always looking at him askance, with a kind of dismissive yet menacing glint in their eyes, but recently he had noticed, generally speaking, that not only his wife but also the few others he knew in his building had begun to act differently toward him, as if, inadvertently and unwittingly, he now made them openly uneasy. It was partly because of this, because of them, that the "cloud mountain" was acquiring such terrible importance for him; and it was likewise because of them that he neither dared nor really wanted to stop interpreting its vague prophesies.

Somewhere far away, deep in his memory, there still occasionally flickered the image of a valley that must have once been his home. But he couldn't remember if, back then—or rather, back there—he had been able to see any mountain. Maybe. But everything from his childhood was such a blur it couldn't possibly have any definite meaning for him, and indeed, these fragments, the hazy outlines of that valley, instead of being part of some actual but distant past, might just as easily be the remnants of a dream . . . Then, too, there would be thoughts about animals descending in packs from the beauty and silence of the mountain, down and down, every day hurrying again into the valley; mostly they were goats, great black herds of goats, so that nearly the entire mountainside appeared soft and undulating with their figures. And when in the morning a flock of pigeons would fly over the rooftops and between the apartment towers and then veer sharply just beneath the "mountain," as if fleeing something . . . it couldn't bode well at all. Folds and furrows beneath the upper "crest" of the "mountain" were also serious warning signs. If there was a kind of hump on the "ridge," then he had to close the curtain halfway, light up his pipe at once, and all through the day, whenever he came to a door, stand for a moment in front of it and say to himself: "Everything will be fine, it will be all right"—and so dispel the nagging fear that the very next moment something terrible might happen, a catastrophe. Even at home, if he wanted to go from the kitchen to the living room or the bathroom, each time he would have to stand for a moment thinking, until he had a clear feeling of confidence—confidence in the strength of his heart and in the purity of his thoughts—and all this would have to be concealed from his wife or, indeed, from whomever might be watching him. And then, more than once, a shape had appeared in the cloud that looked like the face of some divinity. He detected contours seeming to delineate meekness, benevolence, grace; and if below, among the "foothill" clouds, the red traces of dawn radiated out in narrow beams of light, then he knew which shoes he must put on, which shirt he must wear, and which, too, was the proper necktie (in any case, it was the one he invariably wore on days when the cloud couldn't be seen), and, instead of goats, it was better to think about white, freshly washed sheep, ewes with two little lambs apiece, grazing peacefully under a steep cliff.

2

This morning, too, that is to say, the morning when the newspapers delivered the news about the murder in Brežine, he was, pipe between his teeth, observing the "mountain" glowing against a sky that was still a somewhat nocturnal blue. At the same time, the remnant of a familiar half-dream was again, with its usual pain, weaving through his thoughts: most often he seemed to hear a voice, not his wife's, but a sort of childish singsong calling to him, or maybe just singing, which in the morning when he woke up always left him with an anxious sense of emptiness. And when the "mountain" had settled and the first gleaming rays of dawn fanned out red through layers of reaching cloud, he was once again filled with anxiety about the awakening day and the people on the street and the puffs of steam and the city, which was slowly, lazily, opening its hungry maw to devour the herds, and the dreams, and the thoughts, and the startled flock of pigeons above a nearby dome and bell tower. And again he was seized in some deep hidden place by that feeling of needless haste, as if someone—who knows when or where—had commissioned him, commanded him to do something, something important, urgent, and he must set about his tasks without delay, he must get going, must be somewhere—although the "where" and the "why" were somehow always missing; it was as if he heard, echoing in his head, "Go! Hurry!" and this command in itself, without reason or purpose, was enough to send him into the crowd, onto a streetcar, and then anywhere at all, into the rush, maybe with a black briefcase in his hand and certainly with a meaningful, serious expression on his face, going from door to door, wherever there was a sign for a lawyer or notary, stepping into their vestibules and then, a minute or so later, back out to the street and onward, as if he were always a little late, a little concerned, but always, of course, maintaining a façade of importance and dignity. So he shook out his pipe. He dressed in his impeccable gray suit, tied his necktie, put on his well-polished shoes, and hurried to the elevator, glancing a few times at his watch, just like any businessman who knows that time is money; and then down to the foyer of his building, where he nodded in passing, absently and stiffly, to someone leaving for work or wherever else, took his newspaper from his mailbox, and, as if in a hurry, returned to his apartment.

Only later, sitting in his living room in the armchair by the window, his pipe freshly lit, after first taking a look, as was his custom, at the naked girl with the honey-sweet smile in the center spread of the paper, and then immediately, without wasting any more time on trivialities, turning with expert resolve, in a single motion, to the stock market reports—only then did he calm down a little and become more absorbed in his reading, letting his thoughts wander among the submeanings and supermeanings he discerned: opportunities only an expert could spot, and well-concealed traps too, which he of course would never fall into were he ever presented with the possibility. He quite enjoyed this swarm of thoughts, these emerging scenes of his own importance that somehow drew him in, drew him on to acts of heroism, which are of course essential when the data revealed to the public is so very different from the truth, and when one's ship is sailing safely along a well-conceived, carefully charted route, and when little white sheep are floating in a clear sky above puffs of steam, looking as if they had just been washed. Now he turned the page and, just to amuse himself, read about some shady business involving the purchase of some brewery tanks—until a headline in the lower left-hand corner caught his eye: MURDER IN BREŽINE. The article said that the body of Metod Mario Pavlin, a wealthy and respected widower, was discovered accidentally by neighbors in the Villa Carlina, that the death had been caused by an unusually precise "surgical incision" on the neck, and that the initial results of the investigation pointed to murder. In the interests of the investigation, police were not yet divulging any details; nevertheless, they did reveal that, since a number of extremely valuable items, including cash, were left undisturbed, this was not in all likelihood a case of murder for gain. The reporter went on to say that investigators would undoubtedly soon provide a more detailed account, inasmuch as the entire Brežine neighborhood was so profoundly distressed and dismayed by what had transpired.

Valent naturally had doubts about this last point. After all, in a big city like this, reports of murder are, if not everyday occurrences, at least fairly frequent. A person who lives in the same neighborhood where a murder takes place might, indeed, upon hearing such a report, feel a certain distress, might even wonder a little about this or that detail or particularity—but all this, to be sure, is quite removed from any truly profound distress and dismay. While "distress and dismay" might very well characterize the reaction of the victim's friends and relatives, and maybe, too, a very narrow circle of neighbors and acquaintances, for most people, even those living just two or three streets away, the whole affair would be little more than a curiosity, a topic for amusing gossip and café conjecture, which would naturally start losing its titillating freshness the very same day it was reported. And once you crossed the first major intersection on either side of the crime scene, then it would become something entirely impersonal—a serious issue, to be sure, but part of what might be called a bigger problem, at which one could only shrug one's shoulders. And as you followed the streets into the city, the whole thing would gradually become something quite mundane, just gray ordinary reality, of no particular interest to anyone.

For Valent Kosmina, too, this news would no doubt have remained a matter of complete and ordinary indifference had it not involved Brežine, a pleasant, stately district of chestnut-lined avenues, old villas surrounded by noble gardens, and softly lit sleepy streets where he had made it his custom these past few years to stroll, despite the neighborhood being so far away. For it was only in Brežine that he managed to feel, at least to some extent, truly a gentleman, and these evening strolls in his dapper black evening suit were the only thing that made his days complete. He delighted in a certain epicurean tranquility as he walked in elegant attire with calm, deliberate steps beneath the chestnut trees, and many of those he passed must surely have imagined that he himself resided in Brežine. His life would be almost miserable without this feeling of Brežine elegance. Indeed, he loathed the thought of walking through some shabby park like some ordinary pensioner.

Of course, he always made sure his wife knew nothing of these strolls. He made up a story about a group of retired professors and doctors who liked to meet in a certain café—top-notch people, in other words, who expected him to join them more or less every evening. Maybe she even believed it. But in any case, there had recently been no problem at all with him going out in the evening whenever he wanted. She just accepted it. It was fine with her . . .

Last night, too, he had gone for a stroll in Brežine, and this now seemed a rather unfortunate, even somewhat ominous circumstance. He couldn't ignore the fact that, just as on all his other strolls, last night too he had been observed by people who would remember him, who had always taken note of him, and who would undoubtedly be able to give a precise description to police investigators. As, indeed, could any of the staff at the Little Paradise, the tavern where he was, one might say, a regular.

In short, it appeared more than likely that the investigators would take every opportunity to make inquiries at the taverns in the area. Which meant that the waitresses and the two Paradise twins would report him, too—report, that is, his behavior last night, which was perhaps a little out of the ordinary, since he had stayed at the tavern for only a short time—he hadn't felt very well last night—and had barely touched his second carafe of burgundy when, without waiting for the waitress, he shook out his pipe, put a banknote on the table, and left. True, this was not the first time he had behaved in just this way or something like it. But they probably wouldn't remember that now and therefore could easily draw the investigators' attention to him. That would of course be extremely unpleasant for him. Even precarious. For then, undoubtedly, his appearance as a man of means (and, for some, even a resident of Brežine) would soon be exposed as a sham; he would be put in quite a bind, terribly embarrassed and humiliated, at best, before his neighbors and his wife.

His first inclination was to abandon his Brežine strolls altogether, at least for the present, and in general, to keep far away from Brežine.

But it soon dawned on him that such a plan could prove to be a very bad, perhaps irreversible, mistake; that, in other words, this in itself would certainly arouse serious suspicions.

He did, however, find consolation in the thought that they might very soon catch the actual perpetrator, if they had not done so already.

But somehow he couldn't convince himself.

And the more he thought it over, the more everything got tangled in a gloom of uncertainty—an anxiety he eventually managed to curb and contain within himself, but only with a considerable effort that left him with a pain in his stomach.

The morning was already too far gone to consult the "mountain" for help.

He tried in vain to recall if he had ever chanced to see the name "Carlina" on any of the houses in Brežine. Unfortunately, he had never taken much notice of such details. At night that kind of thing is hard to see. And one is not particularly attentive. Moreover, the dusky fronts of the houses are mostly set off a little from the street, behind tall iron fences, and veiled by the shrubbery and trees of the front lawns.

The newspaper didn't name the street or give any more precise time as to when the event occurred. As far as he knew, he could have possibly walked past that very villa every time he took his stroll. If so, then he might have been fairly often seen in its vicinity. Which, of course, is an item of information. Which investigators, of course, would seize upon. Cling to. And the investigating officer, stubborn, taciturn and unflappable, would ask precisely that, about that very thing; he would hardly buy the story about him merely taking a stroll.

As Valent heard his wife moving about—getting out of bed, leaving the bedroom, going into the bathroom, just like any other morning—the pain in his stomach got worse, becoming a kind of chill cramp.

Hastily, he raised the newspaper again. And through the aromatic smoke of his pipe, tried to read something. Anything at all. Tried to absorb himself in reading. To adopt the posture and assume the guise of a man of leisure engaged in his daily routine.

She did not greet him when, in her pink dressing gown, makeup and creams, with a towel twisted around her head like a turban, she entered the living room. She would often come out of the bathroom in just this way, more or less early in the morning, with an almost involuntary scowl on her face. And with a forced cough. Usually he paid no attention to her. But today he wanted to feel that the two of them were closer, friendlier; he would be grateful to her for any sign of intimacy, any show of loyalty, and so despite her silence he said good morning and as a mark of politeness shook out his pipe and put down the newspaper.

She did not respond.

Without a word she went into the kitchen and, from the sound of it, set about making coffee.

At the very least she might have returned his greeting; it would have calmed him down. He wished he could just ask her to please say good morning to him. It would have been a positive sign, and of course it would have made him feel less uneasy; he would have settled down and tried to be sensible about things. But at the same time he had the thought that, even so, he could turn the whole thing to his advantage if, calmly and without a word, he simply went up to her and, right out of the blue, gave her a good smack in the face. He got chills just thinking about it. Nevertheless, he kept on staring at the newspaper, at its jumble of letters and lines of print and columns and pictures, all the while taking slow, deep breaths, silently, so she wouldn't hear, each time holding the air a few seconds in his lungs and then, no less furtively, letting it out. But the letters and lines of print continued to shimmer before his eyes like haze above overheated rooftops.

Without a word she brought him coffee. And with her own cup in hand went and sat down, coughing, in front of the television set.

Rather reluctantly, he mumbled a "thank you." And without lifting his eyes, opened the newspaper. And turned immediately to the next page. And found himself gazing at the face and the nakedness of a black-haired little girl (that is, she was not much more than just a little girl) who smiled an artificial smile beneath an article about fashion design.

Although her hair and makeup were meant to be seductive, she was nevertheless still childlike, still just a little girl.

But as annoying as it was to look at this girlish body and this, as it were, willing invitation on the face of a child, it was no less annoying to have to listen to the television, which his wife had turned on. To hear that maudlin soap-opera music amid the roar and crash of ocean waves. Which were probably meant to indicate the unpredictability of life or even to be a metaphor of that which, day after day and night after night, rocks and tosses the destinies of men and women. But now as he drank his coffee, he felt another particularly unpleasant stab near his heart. Recently, this had been happening rather frequently as he drank his morning coffee, even when he was not upset . . . As if to console himself, he tried imagining how he would appear, if need be, before the interrogators—what reserve, what cool magnificence he would display, how impeccably he would stand when they ordered him to stand, or if they said to sit, would sit; how he would tell them all, directly to their faces, clearly and distinctly with absolute and dignified composure, that, yes, his life, like most people's lives, was a lie . . .

From the television came the tearful voice of a woman in love calling out desperately to some León, who, however, did not respond.

Of course the interrogator would be sarcastic and rude and even use threats; he would roll his cold, steely eyes; and the faintly etched grimace on his meticulously clean-shaven, pampered face beneath his waxy bald scalp would express just enough contempt to say it all.

Which would show him to be, wholly and consistently, a true *inspector*, one who had mastered every nuance of procedure, who knew by heart the best way to get at the facts. And who of course despised even the slightest attempt at dissemblance . . .

The television music rose and fell and rose and fell, now and then suddenly brimming over, crashing in from the background, then yielding again at the tearful, reproachful sighs and moans of the lead actress, or rather, the lady in the soap opera, whose heart was breaking, obviously because of some trouble with her husband and lover, and who, to judge by the music, had just reached a fateful decision. Waves crashed against a cliff; from the air above or perhaps from the rocks below, came the cries of a seagull, and the lady was sobbing; dark and foreboding depths, as it were, issued forth from the music's intermittent bass. Then, perhaps at the last possible moment, a warm, deep male voice prevented the worst from happening. The lady breathed out, "León!" and a tender, ethereal violin duet began, floating above the bass like gossamer and lingering on even after he replied, "Helena!" Then the waves and the bass and the cries of the seagull gave way to the sounds of gentle, loving gratitude and deliverance. But the very next moment, the city was roaring: the hustle and bustle in the street, footsteps, voices, impatient honking from what must be a traffic jam, and the distant wail of emergency sirens, maybe the police. The slaughterhouse smoke and the derelict buildings couldn't be heard. To judge from the soft clink of a coffee cup, his wife, in the ensuing interval with its portrayal of mundane reality, had helped herself to a sip of coffee. Of late she had often seemed like some alien creature to him. She had even stopped cooking. She was, she said, quite happy with the food from the pensioners' meal service; they fixed very hearty meals; and moreover, it really didn't pay to cook for just two people. She had waited long enough, she said, to at last be able to devote a little time to herself. And if he didn't like it, then *he* could very well do the cooking. No, that's okay, he said, and had no other comment. And he was pleased once again with the way he had shown himself to be a master of forbearance, of superior indifference, and the cool, unruffled countenance—a master, in short, of all the skills that characterize the gentleman, the leader, who in his elevated view of things pays little regard to mundane detail. Even, of course, if only outwardly . . . But that's the way it is, he would tell the interrogator, for the love of God, Inspector, that's just the way it is and there's nothing here for you to wonder at. Everyone strives higher, seeks greater importance, wants to rise to the top, Inspector; we all want to reach the top—what else? At this point, the detective would probably interrupt him. And maybe mention the scalpel . . . yes, he would definitely bring up the scalpel. But Valent would remind him of the saying, never yet proven wrong, that "clothes make the man," and would remind him, too, that there are many different kinds of tops one might strive for and many different paths that lead to them.

The music from the television set rose again and, somewhat jerkily, blended with the rumble of a car.

Then the doorbell rang.

Again, anxiety pounded at his heart and pierced his thoughts. There was a buzzing in his ears. But he managed to compose himself.

He did not lay aside the newspaper. He did not get up. To all appearances, he took no notice of the doorbell, though it rang a second time, now sharper and more persistent. He clung to the thought, as to a life preserver, that even if they were now coming to take him away, there was nothing anyone could actually do to him.

At last his wife, with a reproachful sigh as if to say *he* could have moved his behind, shuffled sullenly to the door.

A shudder passed through the newspaper, and through his thoughts. He'd stand right up, he decided, if they asked for him in that dry official tone they had. And walk right over to them. And look them straight in the eye with a calmly superior, inquisitive gaze. And wait for them to tell him what they had to tell him. And perhaps he would say, "Please, gentlemen, do come in."

His wife opened the door.

Without saying anything.

He held his breath, listening; silence emanated from the hallway—and from between the lines and columns of print, and from the sweetly willing, childlike black-haired girl below them.

He detected a slight uncertainty in his wife's voice when, after a short time, she said, "Hello."

A man mumbled something.

"Yes, that's fine, I'll take it." She was already more at ease.

Then there was the clatter of a lid and now he could hear, quite clearly, the familiar voice of "Mr." Mario (as he was called), who was asking if her husband might be at home.

"He is, yes," she confirmed curtly.

Valent was troubled, even a little baffled, by the reticence of his wife's reply. Her manner with this "Mr." Mario had always been rather casual before, even sugary. But possibly her change in tone could be put down to the soap opera's influence, or perhaps it was only irritation at having to leave her TV program. He tried to dismiss it blithely as a trivial detail, but it was nonetheless peculiar that this "Mr." Mario—who, after all, had once been nothing but a street-corner pornography peddler and now was merely the deliveryman for the pensioners' meal service—should be asking about her husband. And should even say that he'd like a word with Mr. Kosmina, or rather (the man ventured to add, in a somewhat confidential tone), that he had something to ask him, if he wouldn't mind.

"Mr. Mario would like to ask you something . . ." she mumbled, so off-handedly he could barely hear her, then hurried to the kitchen with the meal service's combination trays and some sort of package.

But once in the kitchen she said in a louder voice directed toward the door: "Just go right in."

"Oh, no, no," said "Mr." Mario, declining the invitation. "It's just a small matter. Perhaps if Mr. Kosmina might be so good as to . . ."

Valent reluctantly put down the newspaper and stood up. Then, looking as if he had just been disturbed from some important work that demanded all his concentration, he went over to his harasser. Who, as soon as he saw him, stepped back meaningfully, further into the hallway, obviously expecting Valent to follow without hesitation.

"May I help you?" Valent demanded dryly, and stood right where he was as if he saw no reason to cross the threshold.

But to his astonishment, the little worm—a skinny and strangely pallid man with shallow eyes, who had obviously spent a good part of his life tending to his now-gray little mustache and forelocks—gestured for him to come closer, as if it concerned some confidential matter that must at all costs be kept secret from Valent's wife.

Valent was tempted to just turn around and leave him standing there.

His wife could be heard rattling dishes in the kitchen.

"Mr." Mario, too, as if in a hurry, listened to the noise in the kitchen. Then from the pocket of his white work coat he pulled out a bright pink envelope. He looked it over quickly, one more time, as if to make sure it was the right one, then held it out to Valent with a meaningful, confidential grin. "It's for you," he whispered. And came no closer. The rascal's shameless innuendo couldn't be missed. He even winked and nodded, perhaps as a sign of some exclusive masculine bond between the two of them, as Valent stepped forward nevertheless and casually took the envelope. Then, feigning a mildly inquisitive nonchalance, he read his name in the lower right-hand corner. He thought he detected the fragrance of some fine, sweetly heavy perfume. But in front of this former pornography peddler and current pensioner-meal deliveryman, he had no wish to display anything other than an indifferent acquaintance with such trivialities, concerning which, in any case, gentlemen of his ilk did not share confidences with anyone. So once more ignoring the man's meaningful grin, Valent simply said "thank you" and left "Mr." Mario to think whatever he wanted while he waited to collect his trays. It wasn't until he had returned to the living room, shut the door behind him, and checked to see that his wife was not watching from the kitchen, that Valent quickly folded the envelope and stuck it in his pocket.

On television, meanwhile, there was some sort of quarrel. From the sound of it, someone was even slapped. And over the soft sobbing that followed, his wife was thanking "Mr." Mario for yesterday's spinach side dish.

What Valent most wanted to do, if anything, was show the two of them, as they stood there in the doorway, just a fraction of the contempt he felt for them.

But instead, he simply picked up the newspaper as if he couldn't care less. And turning the pages, perhaps more noisily than necessary, he tried not to think about the stabbing pain in his heart and the perfumed letter.

His wife didn't say anything, didn't ask anything, as she returned to the television; her main concern, it seemed, was whether she had missed anything important.

3

The episode came to an end, but it was not until the music had completely died away and the crashing waves abated that his wife turned off the TV and, as if tacitly resigned to the suffering that was the lot of women throughout the world, went into the kitchen. The envelope in his pocket was still just as fragrant as before, and Valent worried that his wife, too, might smell the perfume. It would be difficult to explain. The fact that "Mr." Mario had handed the thing to him behind her back, and that he himself had then concealed it from her, was not something she would take lightly.

It was of course particularly hard for him to control his own curiosity about what it all might actually mean. It appeared to be some cheap "romantic" proposition, one that must therefore involve the basest sort of procurement—but curiosity has always been a fatal human flaw and Valent was now doing his best to resist it. And to resist any illusion about such matters as well. So he made up his mind to simply flush the thing down the toilet without giving it a second thought. And then forget about it.

But now, with that jarringly raised note of orderliness in her voice, his wife was calling him to lunch. She was already by the entrance to the kitchen, and with her wide, dull eyes beneath raised eyebrows, was silently reproaching him for making her wait, especially since, just as every other day, she had had to prepare the meal entirely by herself. The truth was that he could barely find the patience day in and day out to put up with her and her inevitable mealtime faces, by means of which she tried to display, even after their two boys had left home, a sense of dignity, her dedication to hearth and home or what have you, and maybe even a certain soap-opera decorum, which at some point she had made her own and which decreed that a husband and wife should sit down nicely together around a well-laid table, that each of them should take the cloth napkin standing in the napkin holder, unroll it, and place it next to his or her plate, and that the husband should fill the water glasses from a pitcher especially for that purpose. Only after she had said "thank you" in a seemingly insouciant, elevated tone, usually with a feigned smile, and he had answered "you're welcome"—only then, could the soup be served from the rather kitschy tureen in the middle of the table.

All this affectation would sometimes literally turn his stomach. And the mere thought of that invariably mushy, insipid pensioners' food was, one way or another, profoundly repugnant to him.

"It seemed to me"—she was looking at him from beneath her raised eyebrows as if there were cause for concern—"that Mr. Mario was acting a little strangely earlier."

"I didn't notice anything," he brushed her off abruptly, and slurped up a spoonful of greasy, oversalted soup with a deliberately loud noise.

"It made me think"—she glanced toward the door as if caution were necessary—"he might have a double . . ."

"Now, really . . ."—he persisted in dismissive indifference and, as if concerned mainly with finding something palatable, trawled his spoon through the murky soup.

"I think . . ."

"Good to have you thinking," he broke in, and was unable to resist darting her a look. Then he pushed away his soup bowl.

He knew she was hoping, with those dull, reproachfully glaring eyes, somewhat deadened from her morning tranquilizer, that he would send another such look her way; he knew that her spoon still hovered motionless at her lips. But instead, he simply helped himself, very casually, to the roast and vegetables, and then started ransacking (that's the only word for it) the food on his plate. In fact, he felt a strange, almost giddy merriment about his behavior. And at the thought that she'd be taught a lesson—since decorum required that she now decant the zincky mixture in her spoon noiselessly into her mouth—he could barely hold back a spasm of something like laughter. It even occurred to him to wish her "bon appétit" with an indecorously large chunk of goat meat in his mouth and to screw up his face, full mouth and all, into a big display of teeth, like people on television, in lieu of a smile.

This same toothy display gave him particular pleasure when his wife finally composed herself. She had apparently decided on a strategy of offended, disdainful silence. A strategy of contempt.

And it gave him pleasure once more as she chewed her decorously small bites of food with an expression of sober calm, and merely looked through him, pompously, with big bulging eyes, like an enormous hamster engrossed in feeding.

"I'm seeing Professor Pavlovski tonight," he remarked, as if he had noticed nothing odd about any of this, as if he were just resuming the conversation after a short pause, after exchanging his plate of roast and flavorless string beans for the dessert. Heedless of his wife's deafness, he went on to say, meaningfully, that he and the professor would be discussing the concept of the mathematical zero, which of course was merely a generally accepted postulate, a sort of curious religious dogma designed for everyday plebeian consumption.

"If, let's say, you imagine life as a mathematical equation . . ." She stood up. She did not want to imagine anything. As if in a rush, she cleared away her plate and the soup tureen and the serving platter. And went into the living room. And turned on the TV. "Well, now really . . ." he mumbled, as if in reproach—and in fact he did feel a genuine need for somebody to listen to him, to understand him, somebody he could even tell about the goats and the sheep and the pigeons, somebody he could talk to, freely and fearlessly, about the murder in Brežine and the scented letter, which, perhaps, he might not throw away after all, at least not right now, no, certainly not immediately—that is, not until he had consulted the "mountain" about what to do. Now that he was again able to light his pipe in peace and give the matter more thought, things no longer seemed quite so cut and dry. Especially the perfume, which still penetrated his nostrils so insistently, so subtly, even through the tobacco smoke. The fragrance now seemed strangely enigmatic, as if hinting at something extraordinary. Even calamitous, perhaps. One never knows, after all. One cannot be certain of anything. Not even one's own heart. Not even the zero at the end of the equation, Doctor Professor Pavlovski, or Pavlič, or Pavlin, or whatever you want to be called, whatever you take yourself for—he would tell him—you who are even now on the way down, descending into the valley, just like one of those goats. Only with this difference: for as long as it lasts, you must remain upright and dignified. At least outwardly. What I'm talking about, my dear Professor, is this going-down, this not-knowing. That way, anything can be put up with, at least for the time being. And one can even appear noble, despite all this perfume.

In the meantime, he still felt that horrible stabbing near his heart, and again the sounds from the television set penetrated his hearing; this time, apparently, it had something to do with the murder of a wealthy single woman, and there was something going on between the sister and the lover of the murdered woman . . .

But he was trying to remember if his wife had ever used a perfume that smelled like the scent from the letter. Other women too—even the ones in the brothels he'd sometimes visited years ago. He could almost say for sure that none of them had ever smelled at all like this—so exquisite and aloof, maybe even a little ecclesiastical, and certainly enigmatic, like some sweet-smelling glen that opens up before you and makes you think of myrrh and frankincense and the hidden, perhaps mystical world always hiding behind the visible.

The lover was declaring that in truth he had always loved only her, the sister of the murdered woman. But she hissed back that she hated him . . .

He stood up and, without looking at his wife, went into the bedroom. Obviously, the sister's hatred wouldn't last, and the police inspector would expose the villainous lover just in time, and there would then be one less reprobate in the world.

Sometimes after having his lunch and smoking his afternoon pipe, he managed to doze off. Or at least to succumb, vapidly and without any unpleasant tension in his head, to a gentle reverie where thoughts evaporated in a kind of warm flicker, leaving behind only vague and indecipherable outlines. But now of course, as soon as he shut the door and stretched out on the bed, he took the letter from his pocket and carefully studied the fragrant envelope.

The envelope was unquestionably new. Lightly imprinted on the upper left-hand corner was the image of a lily entangled in thorns, which he had naturally failed to notice earlier in his haste to be rid of "Mr." Mario, just as he hadn't noticed that the margins of the envelope were colored a somewhat deeper shade of pink. There was no visible trace of perfume or any other stain. An envelope of this sort, and so perfumed, might certainly suggest some pleasingly sweet promise, although he was troubled when he saw that, above the full address, which seemed to have been written in a childish or elderly hand, there was no title, no "Mister." This in itself, he thought, was reason enough to reject the letter out of hand, from a most proper and justified sense of aggrieved dignity, or flush it down the toilet unopened. Surely such lack of respect in the envelope's address could mean only the audacity of a pimp. Or primarily that. But after a short while it occurred to him that it might also indicate a peculiar sort of informality, an expression of intimacy, perhaps, or at least a desire for intimacy, and thus a certain personal freedom from established convention—though if this were indeed the case, it would first have to be clear just who the sender was, or at least might be, and what gave this person the right to such exemption. On the reverse of the envelope, which was also edged in a somewhat deeper shade, there was nothing especially noteworthy. And as he folded and fingered the envelope and examined it against the light of the window, Valent couldn't help thinking that it was, in fact, empty. But he could not—he dared not—confirm it. Not until daybreak tomorrow, that is, not until he had looked at the "mountain" and then, on the basis of what he saw, somehow figured out what he should do about all this. For the time being, he had to be content with merely examining the envelope, sniffing it, and trying to unravel the meaning of the thorn-entangled lily. A modest and inconspicuous decoration printed in the same color as the envelope, it appeared at first glance to be rather old-fashioned and somewhat sentimental; but Valent had become accustomed years ago (and even then, a little superstitiously) to seeing or at least sensing in things that were apparently quite clear and unequivocal, something more, something that was, if not actually dangerous, then at least mysterious or ominous, something that filled him with constant foreboding and sometimes painful uncertainty, which he might be able to conceal but could never ignore. In vain he would assure himself that he had no enemies and this was just superstition. But since all those "true beliefs" held by the various societies and sects and congregations around the city, their gods, their truths, and even the belief in nothing, failed to provide him with any satisfactory answer and, taken all together, just made him even more confused, the feeling he had of walking on a thin crust above a dark abyss grew into a more or less constant anxiety that he might, at any moment, plummet. Even the smallest detail could be fateful. He could only wonder that nothing had happened to him yet. And so in what appeared to be merely a decoration on an envelope, he detected, at the very least, a somewhat enigmatic personal mark, the sign of a house or family, or the emblem of some society or organization, to which even "Mr." Mario might belong. Clearly, someone had hired or commissioned Mario to perform this service, probably because they did not want to risk having the letter fall into the hands of his wife if they sent it by mail. He might have asked for—indeed, demanded—a suitable explanation as to the sender before ever accepting the letter. But even now, he thought it probably wise that he had not given "Mr." Mario the chance of entering, in any definite sense, into surreptitious confidences that would, with regard to his wife, be entirely improper.

4

But now, too, he began to succumb to the feeling that he couldn't think anything through, that his thoughts were too stunted, too feeble, to be of use, that they went astray in unreliable and uncertain meanings and couldn't get to the bottom of anything. The letter did indeed stir his imagination, reviving all sorts of images from somewhere in his memory and suggesting scenes with tender young voluptuaries whose pictures he had found in various magazines and who always made him feel one and the same thing, as if each of these pictures contained always the same creature, the same allure that drove men crazy . . . but even these thoughts, these scenes and images, kept slipping away and shifting direction, became twisted and distorted, vanishing as if in the vapors above a voiceless abyss . . . which, if you happen to be climbing a mountain in a roped party, you must forget, and so you tell yourself you are going *down* the mountain, safely and securely, and you pretend to trust this safety and security and try not to cause any problems, since you don't want people to think of you as superstitious or desperate, or to be a nuisance or burden to anyone, despite the stabbing pain near your heart and the fact that your thoughts are merely floating illusions, and even though, in the delirium of pain, you glimpse that absurdity which seems every time to be, uniquely and wholly, your own personal matter.

Even if there are bright-colored tapestries and pictures on the walls; even if the windows are curtained and the floor covered in thick carpet and statuettes of little gods stand around the room in silence; and even if the little satyr on the chest of drawers, his mouth gaping toward the ceiling, seems to be howling wildly with pain or lust, and the little ebony girl behind the china cabinet's ornamental glass, clothed in nothing but apparent indifference, seems frozen in a pose of charmingly coquettish anticipation—even then your thoughts twist a little into nonsense, and beneath them silent terrors are creeping in the darkness. Even when you try to conceal them in the "mountain," they are still there. And you can hear them. Distended and deathly pale, a sort of madness, each one staring out, dumbly. Waiting. And knowing. And every one of them is like death. And then like terror. Sometimes they gather in a circle and just stare. And wait. Sometimes they disappear in the darkness. Sometimes they flutter into your thoughts. And then, holding hands in a circle, they march with slow, inaudible steps. Obviously going nowhere. And perhaps, in the middle of this circle there is a very dim and flickering light. They too know about Brežine. And the letter. He wanted to tell them, to shout at them, that they were merely his own invention, they weren't really there. That he sometimes gave them one sort of shape and, at other times, another sort of shape. But they should know that he gets this stabbing pain near his heart . . . and he doesn't know what it's about. That he would like to talk to them, shout at them, like this, and that talking and shouting like this is, in a word, nonsense, since they are the ones pulling the strings, their will is a silent command, and any one of them can, whenever it wants, just tread upon that thing that is perhaps a dim and flickering light and thus extinguish the "mountain" . . . and that would be it.

"And then you go crazy," he said to himself, as if in jest, and as if by pronouncing this verdict he could, before it was too late, forestall and deflect the thought that when you're dying maybe you don't dream about young girls and maybe you don't think you're going on a holiday. "The mind becomes delirious," he'd read somewhere—and through all the torment of unbearable thirst, the feeling that you're burning up, with all the desperate gasping for air and the ever-expanding weight on your chest, the haze grows thicker and thicker, twisting into a puff of smoke you cannot hold on to, suck in, or inhale, as you shiver from fever and chills at the same time and nothing remains of the outside world. Maybe this is when they come, hunched over, with their jaws hanging low and their cold eyes bulging. And together and separately, they are death; together and separately, horror—and there is nothing you can do to stop that vertiginous fall into the terrifyingly deep and dark silence of being alone.

Maybe.

What was certain was that he again had that horrible dread of expectation, that nervous tension he got before some inevitable event; his heart was beating restlessly, he felt dizzy, and every now and then a kind of dull languor would take over, as if for a moment something in his body had given way and shifted into free fall. He tried to make himself calm down, to think of something soothing. But nothing worked. And the sense he had of some fateful chain of events, triggered perhaps long ago, was suffused with a heavy, nightmarish feeling that he must certainly have enemies out there somewhere and there was nothing else he could do to turn things to his advantage.

And so he lay in bed until evening came, unable to doze off even for a moment, with that stubborn anxiety in his heart, a slight headache, in a state of tension that was like a horrible delirium, and wretchedly upset with himself. He had failed, indeed, to come to terms with any of the problems haunting his thoughts.

But when, lying there in the dark, he eventually made up his mind to go again to Brežine tonight—despite all that had happened—he suddenly felt a sense of almost total relief.

Indeed, a pleasantly relaxing sort of joy took hold of him as he massaged his face with a fragrant protective cream and applied a very thin layer of powder to his spots and wrinkles; it was as if, primarily, this was an act of universal defiance, against everyone and everything, not least of all the residents of Brežine, and their inspectors and policemen to boot. Next he put on the suit he usually wore on his strolls, which was also his best and most elegant suit, and a long, water-resistant overcoat of soft black leather, and a hat that was still almost new. And, with a fine gold stickpin in his necktie and a matching ring on his middle finger, he was already halfway out the door when, like a man who knows his worth, he muttered something to his wife about meeting Professor Pavlovski; she was still just sitting there staring at the TV. He knew she would hardly think it necessary to say anything in reply or even to look at him as he stepped into the hallway, already frowning at the thought of the noise and the smog and the generally unhealthy climate that awaited him outside, as, seemingly vexed at running behind schedule, he purposely neglected (and not for the first time) to lock the door behind him. In the elevator, which he shared with two girls from a floor higher up (presumably students), who were dressed in gaudy colors and wore entirely too provocative makeup, he was well served by his general appearance as a man of class much too preoccupied with important matters to take notice of his surroundings, a person who with a single motion of the arm and a quick glance at his watch knows how to express everything he deems worth expressing in this, of course, poorly maintained and, of course, too-sluggish elevator.

It was not until they reached the sidewalk that the two girls exchanged whispers, coquettishly, as if in love—at a safe distance, as it were. Then having moved on a few steps, they broke out in giggles. Which gave Valent a pang of annoyance and rattled him a little, just as he was rattled by the sight of an undertaker's vehicle in front of his apartment building—surely they could have parked it somewhere else; also the angular silhouettes of the dark buildings towering over him everywhere he looked, with hardly a single illuminated window—these, too, made him uneasy. He could hear the buzz and rumble and hiss of the neighboring streets and boulevards, and now and then the jangle of a streetcar bell, and somewhere a muffled boom from who knows what, and the distant hum, extending further and further outward in circles, was like some horribly suffocating abyss that every so often made him feel faint. The narrow, crooked patch of evening sky above the apartment towers was veiled in a yellow haze. These early evening hours, when the streets were most congested, were almost always stifling. People moved about as if in a daze or a drunken stupor . . . his thoughts mostly hovered hazily in the air, something to do with the obtrusively garish advertising signs and exorbitant window displays; the too-juvenile nakedness in the magazine stands and on billboards; the crammed streetcars; the awful traffic jams by the shopping centers; the weirdly alien dark city corners from which the rabble crawls out at nightfall; the shadowy, rank courtyards, passages, and stairwells hidden behind the building fronts; and the impatient, greedily frenzied madnesses within and among humankind. Also he couldn't help thinking about those two girls (presumably students) and how they had laughed at him. And this gnawed at him, at his guise of upright nobility, as he nevertheless walked on slowly, his hands behind his back and a drooping scowl on his lips, and squinting his eyes contemptuously and slightly lifting his chin, he tried to feign utter indifference to the people rushing past. He did not doubt, of course, that he must even so be attracting people's extremely covert, usually inconspicuous attention. He felt, too, that his dignified, resolute gait clearly set him apart from the others, indistinguishable in all their running about, and that in comparison with him it would be impossible to ascribe even some respectable desire, let alone any truly worthy sentiment, to all these people. It pleased him, with a secret, silent pleasure, whenever someone in the crowd, rushing toward him on the sidewalk, stopped right in front of him and became confused, not knowing in that moment of confusion whether to step to the right or the left. All Valent had to do was stand there. With an air of superiority. Calmly. And simply wait for the other person to somehow orient himself and move out of the space in front of him. He wouldn't dream of stopping like that for anyone. And waiting. And looking into the pale face of some old man, into those seemingly unseeing eyes a few inches away. Only once, years ago, had it happened that he and some woman dressed in mourning had stopped like that, both at the same time, face to face, and she had wordlessly, with nothing more than a piercingly stern gaze and a single imperious gesture, forced him, momentarily confused, momentarily docile, to step out of her way. For a long time afterward he couldn't come to terms with what had occurred and though the memory somehow faded, it couldn't be entirely forgotten. Since then he had in many ways improved his appearance and was now well practiced in the role of the elegant gentleman out for a stroll who commands all possible respect.

Now, as he had often done, he took a shortcut through a somewhat out-of-the-way plaza between now-dark office buildings and went down a narrow set of stairs to the nearest taxicab stand. Where, as usual, he took a cab first to the city center. It seemed to him, after all, that anyone with a little self-respect should stop first in the center of town; he was convinced that only in the city center could he truly rid himself of that suburban apartment-block insignificance, which certainly did not belong in Brežine. So he got out of the cab in front of the dark, dusky building of the central bank and assumed the guise of a culturally aware man of the world—in short, a man filled with inspired, elevated thoughts who has just come from a splendid banquet after an important symposium and, still caught up in all the grandeur, now strolls over to the town hall, where he takes a taxicab to Brežine.

On this occasion, however, the sort of spiritual composure one sees in the self-contented faces of those who have just been in the company of others like themselves did not come to him so easily; at least he felt this was the case, and so too would it probably appear to a well-trained observer. An annoying uncertainty about this evening's stroll in Brežine weighed on his thoughts. It increased even more when, as he sat down in a cab in front of the deserted town hall, he told the unfriendly driver where he wished to be taken and the man looked him over rather suspiciously. Valent had to admit that in all likelihood the actual murderer would behave in just this way, that is, he would try to avert suspicion by acting normally. Then too, as the saying goes, murderers always return to the scene of the crime. The driver continued to scrutinize him once they were on their way; several times he caught the man eyeing him in the rear-view mirror with cold suspicion. After shifting needlessly in his seat and then pressing himself in a corner as if to hide, Valent began to look out the window, feigning a casual curiosity, as if he were primarily interested in observing the traffic and noting the order of the buildings that flashed by along the road. But once again he had to admit that his behavior was exactly like, or at least very similar to, that of a killer, and this was not a good way for him to correct the impression he was making on the cab driver. Especially if, as he was beginning to think, this very same cab driver had driven him to Brežine on some previous outing. Maybe even yesterday. Especially if the man remembered Valent and had made a connection with the report of the murder and so was having certain suspicions that he did not even bother concealing. But just as Valent was beginning to take comfort in the thought that, in a city as big as this, cab drivers were probably unlikely to remember specific passengers, a question from the front seat struck him like a bolt of lightning: "To the Little Paradise, then?"

They were still nowhere near Brežine.

There was no reason for the driver to ask such a question now.

And the question did not at all seem to be merely a question.

"The Little Paradise, yes, well . . . there, yes . . ." To make matters worse, he could barely get the words out. And then, even more awkwardly, he tried to set things right: "So you know about Brežine . . . I mean, you've taken me there before . . ."

The driver said nothing.

It was almost as if the man had learned enough. As if he saw no reason to continue the conversation. After hearing what he had heard. And that was all he needed to know.

Valent felt his throat seize up in frustration.

He wanted to tell the man to stop the car.

But, he thought, that would make it look as if he wanted to escape.

Instead he tried to calm himself down. To stop trembling. And to absorb himself in the hubbub of the city; the street lights; the illuminated signs, most of which featured stylishly dressed or undressed young women; the arcades and columns rushing by; the building fronts and store displays and dark windows; the packed streetcar that had just stopped at a traffic light; the silhouettes behind its misted windows; the train now speeding across the overpass; cars here and there; the gap-like space that held a bit of nocturnal sky, a darkened tower with a sleepy red signal at the top; and then again the store displays . . . More than once, as the car stopped and accelerated and turned, he spotted a hearse—and meanwhile the cab driver, especially at traffic lights, kept brazenly watching him, clearly feeling no need to avert his eyes. A crowd was gathering in a brightly lit square by a caryatid-adorned building—it might have been a cinema or a theater, who could say?—and there were some sleepy apartment towers in the background, with a few trees and a brief patch of darkness concealed by both a concrete fence and a shimmering row of lights . . .

Then it all went away.

As if it was over. The noise, too.

Piercing the now-distant glow, outward and upward in a slowly rotating cone, floodlights from who knows where disappeared into the darkness of the sky. And then, at long last, fanning out in a curve, the Brežine river embankment appeared with all its boats docked, as if asleep, in the marina. And the wide dark surface of the water, lined by the lights of the embankment and their reflections, recalled for a moment the alluringly silent tranquility of the "mountain" above the eastern horizon.

5

Just as every evening, Brežine slumbered in stately remoteness. Softly lit secluded streets, canopied by ancient trees, meandered past villas and gardens; here and there among the ornamental hedges stood illuminated statues and sculptures, looking like something out of a dream; and across an expanse of green lawn, at the intersection of sandy paths, bowl-shaped jets of water cascaded in the soft blue radiance of a tall fountain. And every so often some dark, elegant car would pass along the road.

There were a few people out strolling. But the first thing one noticed about them was their complete lack of haste. It was if a general ease held sway, a kind of soothing certainty, a Sunday-like repose in the secure shelter of centuries-old habits and manners.

It occurred to him that the cab driver probably knew where the Villa Carlina was.

But of course he couldn't ask him.

In the meantime, he noticed three girls walking along the sidewalk, all of them provocatively dressed. One appeared to be not yet an adult; that is to say, she was still just a little girl. While the other two bore a strong resemblance to the two students (as he presumed they were) from the elevator of his building. Even after the cab had left the three of them in the distance and a densely overgrown hedge concealed them from view, they still seemed . . . of course, the cab's headlights had illuminated them only for a moment, and then it had been hard to see them clearly in the streetlight, but he couldn't help noticing the surprisingly bizarre resemblance. It even upset him, reawakening his suspicion that there was a connection between things, a chain of events that directed and guided you so that, without knowing or understanding how, you found yourself in a certain place at a certain time; others might call it coincidence, as if it meant nothing at all. But when he considered that for one such coincidence to occur there would have to be a seemingly endless and, at the same time, incredibly precise sequence of mini-coincidences, he could only sigh and try to steer his thoughts, like heedless sheep getting too close to the edge of a cliff, back to the luxuriant stateliness of the gardens and parks and villas of Brežine.

But now at last the cab driver was pulling the car up to the Little Paradise.

Valent paid the fare disdainfully, without a word, as if he were late for some important meeting. Then he hurried up the steps to the entrance. A gently subdued light bathed the richly sculpted portal in shades of deep bronze as the liveried doorman opened the heavy door with a slight bow.

In the vaulted vestibule, adorned with murals depicting idyllic bowers and sultry, amorous liaisons between gods and specially chosen mortals, the guests of the tavern were met by a pair of red-headed twins. To Valent it always seemed as if they themselves, warm and willing, had just stepped out of the idyllic tableaux on the walls. With hardly a sound, with slight smiles, and with discreetly provocative, perhaps even wild, expressions on their sharply defined features, they now came forward and wordlessly took his hat and overcoat. Even after all this time he couldn't tell them apart. Nor could he detect any difference in their clothes; each wore a long, charmingly diaphanous white dress, high-waisted and loose-fitting, accented by a crosshatch pattern of interlacing blue ribbons that extended downwards from a plunging neckline. And whenever either of them would escort him through the flickering half-light to an empty table, they invariably turned the heads of nearly everyone in the room.

Normally, his manner here would be casual, though in a refined sort of way, as befits a gentleman who, during a stroll, likes to stop and have a drink in a congenial, cozy ambiance. He had even made a habit of nodding slightly toward the other tables—although never once did he receive even the least response to these nods; then, after being seated, he would take leave of his hostess with a playful wink, in a casual, confidential way, as if he were sure all his needs would be seen to.

But tonight he couldn't quite pull it off. He felt himself awkwardly second-guessing every gesture, every thought. Even the act of tamping expensive tobacco in his pipe, lighting it, and expertly puffing out the aromatic smoke somehow failed to impart any sense of security or self-confidence. Glances from the neighboring tables paralyzed him. At least some eyes, he was sure, were resting on him longer than normal. And when the waitress hurried over as usual with his regular half-liter of burgundy, her smile nearly reduced him to pathetic imbecility. And it required some effort to regain his composure. It was only after downing first one and then, straightaway, a second glass of wine that he found the courage to look around. A few of the regulars he knew by sight, though he had never uttered a word to any of them.

For the most part, the other guests were older couples, conversing together in casual or flirtatiously discreet tones, all of which gave him the general impression that last night's murder was no longer a topic of conversation. It was hard to believe that all these smiling faces—pale though they were, but otherwise cheerful or softly amorous, seductive or merely self-satisfied—could be talking about some "surgical incision" in the jugular or the possible perpetrator of the crime, who after all might even be here tonight, hidden behind a well-rehearsed, smiling exterior, and might even be selecting his next victim. A thin haze hovered over the room and its cherrywood furnishings. An aroma of cinnamon, combined with the sounds of a piano, induced a sweet aura of intoxication and reverie. Such a setting, to be sure, made it much easier for Valent to relax and forget himself. But still, tonight, despite the burgundy and everything else, he wanted to remain on guard. Because you can never know for sure. Because you can never be too cautious. And because, ultimately, he still caught a few people looking at him here and there, as if by chance, of course, as if inadvertently.

And so, to all appearances, he was lost in thought, like a gentleman who enjoys the chance to light up his pipe in congenial surroundings and think his own thoughts for a while, quite happy to be left alone, whom nobody bothers with any overt attention or affability. The truth, however, was that he did not feel the least bit sure of anything, especially tonight. He couldn't keep his eyes from darting to this or that table, as he was mainly trying to hear, amid the sounds of the piano and the muffled conversations, whether anyone might be saying anything (covertly and indirectly, of course) that related to him. He couldn't rid himself of the strangely unpleasant feeling that people were really talking about him. Not even the burgundy was helping tonight. And at the next table an old lady with limp curls, dyed a vivid yellow yet so sparse the scalp showed through, appeared to be saying something rather suspicious. She was getting what were clearly nods of sympathy and understanding from her two friends, and all three women had flushed faces. When he finally managed to catch a few words about a cat with diabetes, he smiled to himself—that is, as if he were smiling at some curious notion he had or simply at the wineglass in front of him. And he sat up straighter. And poured himself more burgundy. And did not fail to notice the brief but inquisitive look of one of these ladies, who perhaps wanted to be sure that what she had just heard was really true. Also, at the table on his left, a gentleman approximately his same age—who may, of course, have been merely feigning his interest in a youthful, smartly dressed, and apparently quite amusing blonde woman—was doing his best to conceal a certain impatient awkwardness. And there was a noticeably labored tone in the conversation of a group of rather dandified men in dark suits gathered at a table by the exit. In fact they formed a ring. A semicircle. And the feeling of being trapped between the wall and all these others only increased his anxiety. They could, ultimately, decide not to let him leave, and the covert looks that were undoubtedly being exchanged only deepened his horrible suspicion that there was some connection between them, some agreement—a secret intention, that is, behind this collective camouflage of people merely sitting at a table, engaging in everyday affectation or socializing with practiced nonchalance. One of the elderly ladies at the table on the right mentioned that it would be best to "put him out of his misery" since on top of everything else he was rather old, too. And the other two, it seemed, were tacitly agreeing. He did not dare look in their direction. So they had come to a decision. About the cat, of course. They had sealed its fate. And now they were devoting themselves to their coffee or their tea or whatever it was. And he emptied his glass in a single gulp. And immediately poured himself another. And downed that one, too. And thought he should somehow try to slip away. Should act as if for no special reason he just feels like going. Without finishing the wine. Or maybe he would finish it. But now the sallow-faced gentleman on his left was standing up. And so was the blonde woman. And they both, one after the other, looked in his direction before they left. As if they sensed, or even knew, that he intended to leave right after them. Others, too, might realize and expect the same thing. Maybe they were watching out of the corners of their eyes. Some were, at least. Some of them might even be specially assigned to watch for guests who are acting suspiciously. And it seemed to him that if he were to stand up just now, shake out his pipe, and leave, that would certainly arouse suspicion. So when the waitress came to clear the table of the couple, who had perhaps only seemed to be lovers, and asked him in passing, with the visible beginnings of a smile and in that fashionable Brežine way—that is, in a slow and almost lazy drawl—if "the gentleman would care for anything else," he ordered another bottle of burgundy. When she then returned with the burgundy and once more poured him a glass, the others pretended not to notice and not to care, though he suspected they were actually rather surprised, since they had expected anything but this. All of which, of course, suited his purposes very well, so he promptly tilted back his glass with a flourish.

In fact, in the sophisticated, flickering twilight of the room, he was the only one sitting alone, and this, he told himself, made him look even more like a distinguished gentleman.

In the meantime, they seemed to have turned off some of the lights. The table at the left was now occupied by two self-important men, both rather heavyset. The piano player was now joined by a clarinetist. And every so often, one of the twins (but who could say which?) would appear and circulate from table to table.

Faces seemed made of wax. Eyes shimmered. Here and there, people grinned. And penetrating the vivaciously dense sound of talk, there rose the nasal tones of the clarinet, dreaming and wailing and shrieking and not knowing where to go.

The two fat men at the table to the left were also drinking burgundy. It seemed to him they were just sitting there silently, tipping back their glasses in a strange sort of way, as if their toupees were too tight, and looking around the room. Valent could see the face of only one of them. The other had his broad back to him.

And above that short, stout neck, the toupee was unmistakably tilting a little to the side. He thought he recognized the bull-like hump in those shoulders . . . Two or three times, he found the courage to look straight in the direction of the two men, as if accidentally, and each time he was struck by something almost murderously soulless in the frowning fleshy face he saw. The clinging suit, the buttoned-up collar, and the too-small bow tie beneath an overhanging double chin told him that these two couldn't be from Brežine. So, he thought, some of the rabble has found its way here from their dark holes in the city. He preferred to listen instead to the conversation of the old ladies who, having resolved matters about the cat, had decided to order another round of warm cognacs and were obviously in no hurry to get home. Their conversation dwindled then swelled, faltered and surged again, in a meaningfully excited tone, ever livelier, and finally seemed to find its bearings as something was said about new forms of modern lighting, something about amaryllis, and so on and so forth. And then someone mentioned the "surgical incision" at the Villa Carlina, and the famous Pavlin family opals, of which the elderly Pavlin had made a present to his fiancée "or whatever she was supposed to be"; that allegedly he had confided this to someone, and that later these very same opals were found next to his completely naked body. "At least fifty years have gone by . . ." And the body had been sprinkled with perfume. "Shalimar," added the lady with the yellow curls, as if, indeed, she was well acquainted with the details. And for some unstated reason, she concluded that the murder had been committed by the fiancée, who, however, had never actually been found.

He couldn't hear everything they were saying. He thought about moving his chair a little closer, under the guise of making himself more comfortable, but he was afraid the women would see through this ploy—nor would it escape the fat man facing him, who in fact was observing Valent with an interest he no longer bothered much to conceal. Then, too, he couldn't make much sense, of course, of that "fifty years ago or more." Maybe the women were referring to some other, similar event . . . So the suspect was a woman, a mistress, that is, who perhaps wasn't satisfied just with opals and presumably liked to deliver her revenge with a touch of romance . . . At the same time, Valent was becoming convinced that the fat man facing him was actually mimicking the way Valent was drinking. Earlier there were other moments when he thought this might be true, but now that he began to pay closer attention, purposely raising and lowering his glass a few times, from the corner of his eye he saw that the other man did the exact same thing. One of the old ladies, meanwhile, had mentioned the word "phantom." And Valent turned his back on the fat man, as if to show that such tasteless pranks were beneath him. And in any case, as if in good-hearted fun, he had begun to watch one of the twins, who was wiggling her hips suggestively as she once more made her way past the tables and out of the room. He even smiled. To himself, as it were. That is to say, as if he were simply recalling a pleasant memory. And he started to toy with the notion that one of these evenings he might indeed treat himself to a little bit of dessert with one of the hostesses (as would undoubtedly befit a gentleman of his years) . . . Maybe even with both of them . . . And just as in one of those idyllic scenes, the three of them would nobly go at it into the wee hours of the morning . . . until the first light of day. Until the "mountain."

Afterwards at home he'd somehow manage.

But no matter how he played with this idea, it just wasn't doing the trick.

Not tonight, at least.

The burgundy and the smoke in the room left him with a certain heaviness, an aching in his head, and in his arms and legs, and a tiny sharp burning sensation, like a glowing ember stinging him in the middle of his heart. He tried to forget, to expel from his thoughts, this "fifty years ago or more," and the letter, and the suspicion that it was somehow connected with the perfumed corpses. And he tried to convince himself that this was the most ordinary sort of coincidence. Like countless others that occur day to day. But it wasn't enough to just shrug his shoulders at all the things that today in the city had smelled like Shalimar and yet could have no connection to the murder in Brežine. It wasn't enough. It was as if there was no certainty at all in this kind of reason and logic. He had the disconcerting feeling of being trapped, of being bound up in vague and inexplicable fears by torpid fatigue, that his thoughts were no longer entirely his own and he could do nothing but wait for some voiceless command from something inside himself, which only appeared to be his own thoughts. Whatever it was, this *something* inside warned him to beware of the fat man, and of that still rather restrained group of dandies. The twins too, and the waitress, and even some other guests sitting a bit further away, even the clarinetist—they all seemed suspicious. Naturally he gave no credence to that idle talk about some "phantom." Still, he got a rather unpleasant shock when, at a table not far from the piano player and clarinetist, he suddenly spotted a man who bore a remarkable resemblance to one of his former superiors, whose funeral he had been obliged to attend some ten years ago—as part of the job, so to speak, like all the other underlings. He was also annoyed by the fact that he had failed to notice when the man and woman at another table, apparently some bored married couple, stood up and left.

But as for his former superior, the similarity was certainly unmistakable. Though it might easily be ascribed to some family resemblance rather than anything uncanny.

He was far more upset, even bewildered, when a while later, from the corner of his eye, he caught a glimpse of the table where the two fat men had been.

There he saw, leaning forward and sitting quite alone as if someone had accidentally left her behind, a black-haired girl, not much more than a child . . .

And she seemed oblivious to everyone.

6

In the morning the "mountain" couldn't be seen. The sky was blanketed in a swollen, cloudy grayness, and daylight, it seemed, could barely spread itself across the city. Again, in his uneasy heart, there was an ominous pecking sensation. A dull, throbbing void pervaded his head, which burgeoned with ugly reproaches regarding, among other things, that third bottle of burgundy last night, which was certainly too much and after which he had started losing track of things . . . He couldn't get rid of the feeling that he must have made a truly woeful impression on the people at the tavern, that they had finally caught on to him, and in the end, he had slunk out of the place, humiliated and defeated. He was not even sure he'd paid his tab. He had slipped away, without a shred of dignity or decorum, just like a worthless nobody. And that little girl was sitting there . . . And as he was leaving, one of the twins said goodbye to him with a little smile, flashing her teeth—but no doubt this was simply part of her job.

All the way home, the swarthy fat woman driving the cab had said nothing.

It was true, though, that once he was home, he did sleep better than he had for several nights. But it did him little good. The befogged misery of last night's events still lay there in his aching, tired head like a weight that he couldn't sleep off.

The main thing he felt when he was in such a mood was usually a disgusting sensation of being split in two. This merciless self-censure made him woozy and achy, arousing feelings of guilt, as well as shame and worthlessness—and all of this, as so often before, demanded of him a certain determination. There had been some women, he now recalled, talking about the murder, the "surgical incision," and almost certainly about something else, too—who knows what?—that had gotten stuck in his memory. But when he decided all the same to take another look at that little news item, yesterday's paper was, strangely, not in its usual place. And he couldn't find it anywhere else, either. It was really peculiar. But he had to pull himself together, to calm down. Take a deep breath. Shake out his pipe. And then, slowly, open the letter . . .

It still smelled of perfume.

The image of a perfumed corpse surfaced in his thoughts like a warning.

But he didn't stop. In a kind of convulsion, almost breathlessly, he pulled out a thin, translucent piece of notepaper and read:

Set me as a seal upon your heart!

It was written in a somewhat rusty red . . . like blood. Someone's making a joke, he thought. Yes, someone wanted to make a fool of him; people do this sort of thing to amuse themselves when they're bored. The handwriting was chunky and misshapen. He told himself he wouldn't look too deeply into it, he didn't care in the least; he wouldn't play along with such tasteless pranks. Nevertheless, he spent quite a while examining the rust–colored writing with its shaky lines and uneven loops, curves, and arches, and felt embarrassed about it. He tried to dispel the reproach that he should ever have let Mario give him something so indecent in the first place, and then, that he should ever have opened it. And now, obviously, he couldn't give it back, at least not in its original state. At the same time, he was angry with himself for letting such tasteless nonsense get to him. In fact, everything was making him angry, everything, no matter what he was thinking about. There was also that rather depressing thing in his dreams. It seemed to him that some time in the past, who knows when, maybe even fifty years ago or more, he had taken a wrong turn somewhere; he'd missed some opportunity, and now, if only because of his heart condition, he couldn't do anything differently. This idiotic dissimulation—to himself, to his wife—always having some "errand" to run in the city, or sitting with his newspaper and waiting for his evening stroll, and of course the silent fears, the silent terrors he felt with every step he took on his relentless descent. He crumpled up the envelope. And immediately reached for the note. And again examined it on both sides, at first as if merely with reawakened curiosity but soon feeling mortified about what he was actually doing. And then he no longer knew what he should do . . . and then he lost his courage . . . His head ached with that same old horrible tension. The paper shook in his hand. So he had to fold it carefully and slip it carefully into his bathrobe pocket. It was only the envelope he had to discard, as a small consolation of sorts; he had to flush it down the toilet, and all the while think to himself, over and over: "Everything will be fine. Everything will be fine."

His wife got up early that morning, with curlers in her hair, which meant she intended to go out "on errands."

She even told him this a little later, though he did not actually pay attention to all the things she listed, only that she had "things to do and business to attend to." He wasn't interested. He merely asked her about yesterday's newspaper, but she didn't know where it was. Recently he had felt nothing but growing contempt for all her mundane pensioner's "errands." And the newspaper had just vanished. And she had no idea where it could be. She never read it so why should *she* worry about *his* newspapers, she said on her way out. He suspected that she had thrown it away. And he resolved to tell "Mr." Mario, this very day, exactly what he thought of him and his letter. Disdainfully, of course. He'd even dress up for the part, he decided, and with a well-chosen word or two (in any case, very concisely) would present the very image of dignified determination—which might, indeed, be even more effective at the meal service headquarters, that is to say, in front of the director himself, since a reasonable man, if offended by an obscene gesture, does not, to be sure, address the finger that made the gesture, nor even the hand. He speaks to the head. So of course he would walk straight into the director's office, rigid and serious. And of course would waste no extraneous words on the matter itself. He would not only insist that appropriate measures be taken, he would demand an immediate apology. And then, in the same way, he'd deal with a few other things too. All those insults from the past and all those yet to come. That's right . . . He sat for a while, listening to the more or less painful beating of his heart, mulling over his thoughts, and watching the puffs of steam and the grayness above the eastern horizon, promising himself that he would at last take charge of his life and no longer serve the fears that sought to control him . . .

At some point late in the morning the telephone rang, jolting him out of this headache-inducing, stupefying reverie.

Of course, he'd wait a minute. Of course, he'd take his time in getting up to answer it.

Not until he felt the phone had been ringing just long enough did he pick up the receiver and say, in a lazy, drawn-out voice, as if tired of getting so many telephone calls every day, "Hello-o . . ."

"Good morning," a soft young female voice said in reply. There seemed to be some hesitation, an awkwardness in her voice, and he presumed that in the pause that followed she was trying to compose herself. Quiet music could be heard faintly in the background.

"Hello," he repeated, more curtly now, in a tone of haughty impatience.

"I wonder if I might speak with the lady of the—"

"She's not at home," he interrupted, and sure that this must be just another sales pitch or some similar telemarketing nuisance, he hung up.

These calls always infuriated him. He would simply outlaw altogether these salespeople's invasiveness, hypocrisy, and duplicity. He'd sign a petition in a second, or anything else, if he thought it could put an end once and for all to such audacity, when people have the gall to harass a man in his own home without so much as a by-your-leave and, solely out of the basest commercial greed, disturb his peace and quiet.

Eventually, however, when his anger died down a little, he began to think that the music he had heard in the background was the same as the music last night; that is to say, it sounded as if the duo from the Little Paradise had been playing it. At least there was something very similar about it, something characteristic perhaps—or maybe it was just one of the currently popular tunes that you could hear being played everywhere, which would mean that, like the young female voice, it was just another marketing gimmick. This explanation, indeed, seemed reasonable enough to let him rather quickly dismiss any connection with last night's outing or the Little Paradise, and once again succumb slowly to his earlier reflective mood, which, though it gave him a slight headache, was otherwise not too taxing.

Around noon—that is, a little before the time "Mr." Mario usually showed up—there was another ring.

This time it was the doorbell.

He had not yet actually worked out the speech he would use to call this "Mr." Mario on the carpet for distributing this anonymous rubbish, but he certainly intended to bring up the director and standard business ethics. Now he was sorry he had flushed the envelope down the toilet. The note alone no longer seemed like firm enough evidence. After all, "Mr." Mario could very well say he had never given such a note to anyone.

The man had the audacity to ring the bell a second time—which again gave Valent a start, and again made him swallow some of his rage. But as always, he wrapped himself in a guise of decorous composure and went, slowly, to the door.

Through the peephole he saw a girl in provocative makeup.

It was one of the girls from higher up in the building.

Presumably a student, only now she was wearing a tight wine-colored suit. On her cap, perched a little to the side on top of her long dark-brown hair, he recognized the familiar green logo of the pensioners' meal service.

She smiled at the peephole.

"Good morning, Mr. Valent," she said before he even opened the door. That young smile made a positive impression. And when she stepped right into the apartment and, brushing past him, carried the meal trays right into the kitchen, her air of familiarity seemed perfectly natural and not in the least annoying.

A pleasant fragrance lingered after her . . .

He should probably say something, but at the moment he could think of nothing appropriate. So with a veneer of restrained calm, he just followed her in silence and stood at the entrance to the kitchen.

"It's very nice here. What a lovely smell!" She continued to smile as she sniffed with apparent delight the tobacco smoke hanging in the air and cast a glance at the curtains and walls. And at the very next moment, she looked into his eyes. Directly. And didn't look away. Not for a few seconds. She's a lively little vixen, he thought, and obviously knows her way around people. There was something quite girlish about her. And at the same time, something of the experienced, maybe even debauched woman. He thought of asking about "Mr." Mario. She was certainly a pleasant substitute . . . but now she gathered up yesterday's trays, already washed and ready, and slipped past him, and as she did so, grazed him slightly with her hip. Petite, playfully beguiling, with the devil in her eyes . . .

"Goodbye," she said. And through the half-closed door, wordlessly, mischievously, she leaned back into the apartment and, after a play-fully meaningful pause, as if wanting to say something important, wished him "bon appétit."

Something empty, desolate, remained in the apartment when she finally closed the door and left. He sighed. And instantly felt there was something foolish, even impermissible, in sighing like that after little girls who, perhaps, were only having a bit of playful, innocent fun.

7

It rained several days in a row and from time to time the foggy grayness veiled even the apartment block settlements in the eastern districts nearby. In the evenings, Valent couldn't help missing Brežine, but still he stayed home; the very fact that the "mountain," especially now, was so persistently hidden by clouds made him depressed and uncertain about things. The newspapers no longer wrote about the murder. Nevertheless, he felt nothing but regret for his most recent Brežine outing—which he had undertaken without consulting the "mountain," on his own initiative, as it were. He was still haunted, still oppressed by the feeling that on this last excursion he had profoundly jeopardized, if not utterly ruined, his Brežine reputation—all the dignity, all the nobility of the image he had spent so much time constructing and perfecting and Brežinifying. There was still too much about that night that remained unclear in his memory, which most likely meant he had lost control of himself. Yet out of this disturbingly face-reddening uncertainty, this blurriness, he could still make out something that was sufficiently dubious, even ignominious, which of course others would have noticed, too, people who are normally admirable and, therefore, sensitive—they always see more, much more, than you want them to see. And if the mask falls off, they instantly trample it underfoot; they instantly deride and mercilessly persecute he who is now exposed and ostracized.

This depression, these worries, were also why he avoided a second encounter with the new delivery girl from the meal service, and why he didn't pay much attention at first to the scraping and scratching noises coming from the apartment next door, noises his wife simply refused to hear. It did seem somewhat unusual, however, the way these noises would occur only for a short time and then at peculiar intervals, but this was how things were in an apartment building. "What can you do about it?" he mumbled with a shrug and, much earlier than usual, got ready for bed.

But this *thing* from their neighbor's apartment was far more annoying in the bedroom than when he had heard it in the living room through the sounds of the TV. At first it seemed as though a bird was pecking on the bedroom wall from the other side, at sometimes shorter, sometimes longer intervals. Then it seemed as if something kept on scratching and scratching, with tiny but hard and sharp claws, in a kind of circling or swirling pattern, and then came the pecking again, and then it all stopped . . . He told himself not to pay any attention to this *thing*, whatever it was. And in the glow of the bedside lamp he took another quick look at the perfumed note, then turned out the light. And shut his eyes. And repeated to himself that everything would be fine. And tried to forget all these thoughts about Brežine, and the new delivery girl, and the perfume; to cover them up, shut them out, and come to terms with things, even with his possibly diseased heart, even with himself—that is, with the self that was somehow unsatisfactory, and with the other that would be satisfactory if it only existed in the way the unsatisfactory self existed, if only it wouldn't be so nagging, so judgmental all the time, if only it could somehow be the way it could never be in reality—that is, he tried to come to terms with his double, his triple, or however-many-times-multiple self. Behind closed eyelids the usual spots took shape, the usual (though always new, always different) contorted faces. And he wished he could tell himself: calm down, get a grip on yourself, pull yourself together—and he would tell himself this, of course he would, if only he knew who was doing what to whom and from where and for what reason and for whose benefit it really was and for whom it was intended. He would tell himself: the city is humming down below, as if from far away, from behind a heavy curtain, muffled in the hazy glow of thousands of lights; the television is muttering and sputtering through the door, through the walls; and something is picking and pecking at the bedroom wall, clickety-clacking into my thoughts, whimpering in my ear, scratching in circles, in swirls, with sharp little claws or who knows what . . . He would tell himself this, and then something else, and after that, something else again; and he would sleep and dream of a black-haired girl, not much more than a child, in a light pink skirt with playfully coquettish eyes who would lead him, beckon him, uphill, up some long and unfamiliar street—of course, he might ask himself what it means, just as, *of course,* tomorrow he would tell his neighbor to stop this pecking, this scratching of little claws, since he is not the only one, after all, he isn't alone, and you need to show a little consideration—as you go on up the street and don't know where or why, as this much-too-young but still very nice, very sweet-smelling black-haired little girl with a stickpin that looks like a long thin golden needle in her straight, silky-smooth, shoulder-length hair takes him by the elbow and hurries him along; and he has no idea where they're going, where she came from, or what she wants from him. But he likes it; it's so nice the way they're walking together, the way she sometimes encourages him with those azure eyes of hers.

He doesn't recognize the street they're climbing; it seems they are in some out-of-the-way district. A warm, light breeze blows toward them, and the little pink skirt flutters and catches between her legs, and the monotonous everyday hum of the city recedes farther and farther behind them.

"Are you afraid of me?" she asks, smiling, and he thinks to himself that she is wearing a rather sweet perfume and her complexion is rather more pale than not, and that combined with her azure eyes it creates a somewhat unusual contrast with the black hair and eyebrows. In fact, he has no idea how to answer her question, nor does he intend to. It occurs to him that the few people they had encountered on the street farther back, who without exception had all been going downhill, were now suddenly gone, and the two of them were completely alone, and that this was not an answer, neither for him nor for her.

"Are you one of those who come from the mountain?" he asks her instead, and because she cocks her head only seemingly in reproof, because at the same time she smiles and winks at him, the question appears to please her. So he stops worrying. And listens to the wind and the silence amid the yellow buildings crowded together on either side of the street, and to the girl's footsteps, to the sound, that is, of her heeled, studded sandals, and stares at the gentle undulations in the curved pattern of the granite stones beneath their feet. The cobblestone street reminds him of fish scales. And he likes the thought of walking on a fish; it amuses him, refreshes him in the hot breeze amid the monotonous yellow of these graceless, drab buildings that look like army barracks.

"There's no need for you to be afraid of me," she tells him after a while, as if she had given it much thought, and perhaps also as an answer to his question about coming from the mountain. But now she looks at him more seriously, almost as if in admonishment. A few steps later, however, she is again soft and friendly and girlish. She even seems in love with him as she leans on his arm, tiny as she is, her hip brushing against him as they walk.

The sky above the rooftops is gray and the sun is like honey— maybe old, or maybe it just seems that way because of the wind and air from below; and indeed, the street is like a tunnel through the honey-grayness, a tunnel that perhaps never ends.

"How beautiful your footsteps are in sandals," he whispers to her. He feels a little embarrassed, but he whispers it for his own sake, too. And he would like to add that the world is beautiful solely because of little girls. But at the same moment it occurs to him that a man of his years walking arm in arm with such a child must be careful. Must be reserved. So this walking together doesn't trip him up. So being alone like this with her doesn't dissolve altogether in rancid pain. It's best, then, not to say anything. To be like some not very demanding tourist. Like a tourist who, if nothing else, can feign just the right degree of curiosity and anticipation.

"My beloved is white and ruddy . . ." she says with a confiding, sidelong smile.

It was a beautiful smile.

But then it dawns on him that he is not the one she's thinking of; she can't be referring to him, since, after all, he's not "white and ruddy." So he does not return her smile but instead keeps silent, and somehow feels unsure, doubtful . . . Meanwhile, there's no sound to be heard, no sign of life at all, from the long rows of mainly four-story buildings on both sides of the street. From time to time a window shutter flaps in the wind, but otherwise, except for the echo of her sandals on the cobblestones, a sepulchral silence lies all around, a silence no longer disturbed by the distant hum of the city.

The houses get smaller and even on the outside seem unpleasantly gloomy.

Increasingly he feels the absence of other people. And there is a prickly dryness on his palms, and in his mouth and throat, maybe because of the wind . . . Ugly cracks are showing on the façades of the buildings, between the shattered or even dug-out windows, and some of the rooftops look horribly ravaged while others have already caved in. And it all seems somehow to be staring at them, waiting, and above all, hostile.

The silence all around feels alien and somehow treacherous, and the girl is much too quiet and too much in a hurry, so he tries to resist her, to slow down his pace, but she takes no notice and just pulls him on after her . . . and she doesn't say or explain anything at all, until finally, far from any other people, far from the hum of the city, after looking back down the street a few times as if for no apparent reason and glancing to her right and her left, she turns into a deserted, cluttered courtyard. Only now, in this place, does she raise a tiny finger to her crinkled, pursed lips and whisper, promisingly, as if to cheer him: "I took off my dress . . ." Which of course isn't true, which of course is a lie—perhaps a childishly perverse hint as to what will come later, when they'll be somewhere else, past the tumbled bricks and boards and piles of discarded trash and timber, somewhere she would clearly like to take him as soon as possible. He thinks he sees, near a pile of trash, sticking out from beneath an overturned, rusted-out bathtub, the sandal-clad foot of a woman, apparently dead. Of course he wants to stop. Of course he wants to be sure. To show her. But she's not interested. She doesn't want to see it. As if neither of them should really care. And so using all his strength, he somehow manages to extract his arm from her grip and starts running through the courtyard, and he has no idea why he doesn't go straight to that bathtub or turn back on to the street and down to the hum of the city, which might rescue him, to the bustle, which might save him, where he might simply lose himself, drown in it, succumb to it, let himself be carried, be taken, to wherever it might take him; he has no idea, and just runs recklessly across the broken glass, jumping over bricks and discarded doorjambs and wooden beams, running alongside the high wall of the courtyard (though she isn't running after him), and then somehow he squeezes himself through a low and narrow little door and is suddenly in a large, dark room, a great chamber where he cannot see very well and has to feel his way through the wine-colored gloom, moving between beds and touching the damp, sticky-stained quilted bed covers, which are also lying on the floor and beneath which something occasionally moves—or at least so it seems, as he walks over them with numb and heavy feet and wants to get as far away as possible, as quickly as possible; but for all their softness, they are an extremely irritating obstacle, and this is the real and most immediate problem, since there is no end to them, since in some places they're layered one on top of another and he has to push the beds apart, and every once in a while he has to scramble over piles of all sorts of other needless discarded bedding . . . and on the walls of the chamber there are pictures, each a little crooked, of naked little girls. They seem to have been cut out of various newspapers, periodicals, and pornographic magazines . . . He can't help noticing the shadowy azure in their many eyes, which follow him as if they were alive. And all these pictures of naked azure-eyed girls are, unquestionably, *her*. And only her. There can be no mistaking it. No mistaking, either, the fact that this chamber goes nowhere . . . He can't even find the little door he squeezed through to get in. And wherever he looks it seems as if she has just now, this instant, hidden herself, slipped out of sight, and he can still hear a rustle, still smell her honey-sweet fragrance—and there can be no doubt that she is near. Watching him. Playing a game with him. When all he can do is keep looking over his shoulder, keep searching for that damned little door, which he might be able to escape through after all.

"Here I am," she suddenly whispers, suddenly breathes on him from behind. So that he jumps. Freezes. And he can't help trembling as he now feels her against his lower back, naked, pressing

herself to him, giving herself to him. He has no idea when he came
to be without his shirt and jacket. But now he definitely feels her
against his skin. And the small, barely budding breasts pressed
low against his back are definitely pleasant. "Here you are, you're
mine," she breathes in a whisper and slowly licks his back with her
hot tongue, "in my temple . . ." and he feels her little belly expand-
ing and contracting excitedly, with her every breath, against his
buttocks . . . and her slavering tongue slithers up his back and her
fingernails drag tantalizingly across his stomach and lower down,
and in her confused whispers about her temple, about her prayer,
her lust grows more and more, and she somehow turns him around
and lays him on his back on one of the quilts, and she straddles
him and slowly crouches down on him, whispering, muttering as
if praying, but at the same time there's a whistling in her throat,
as if from a wheezing flute . . . He cannot listen, there's no time
now, because he cannot get himself out from beneath her, because
he's tugging in confusion at the tangled bed sheets, pulling them
off, pushing them away, in every possible direction—damn them
all—because something's gotten twisted, something's gotten stuck,
knotted, and won't do what he wants, won't give, and now his shirt
or something is in the way, but she pays no attention and keeps her
eyes fixed on his, ecstatically, raptly making those whistling noises,
as she takes the sharp stickpin in her hand and draws it in circles
across his tingling nipple and around it and those tangled sheets
and his shirt are getting more and more horribly in the way . . . and
suddenly a sharp pain. Like a thin flame. Shooting through him.
Piercing him. Under his nipple.

Into his heart.

He might have cried out. Or maybe not. His wife, at least to judge from her deep, even breathing, heard nothing. His heart was still racing a little, to be sure, but that piercing, thin sharpness had now almost completely disappeared, as had the girl, and the chamber, the bed covers, the nude pictures, and those strange wheezing-whistling sounds in the dense dark-red gloom. He tried to understand it, to summon it back to memory, but it had evaporated, withered away, and now, no more than a second after he had perhaps cried out and opened his eyes in his own bedroom, now it undoubtedly meant something else.

Once more he was sure he had dreamed of such a girl, perhaps the same girl, a number of times before—and the notion that this girl must, then, somehow be real, must somehow exist and from time to time enter his dreams, though how or from where he couldn't say, stayed with him like a nagging riddle that despite his undoubtedly keen powers of reasoning was beginning to take on an utterly perplexing significance. Of course he would have preferred to simply tell himself that a blue-eyed girl like that might simply mean a blue-eyed girl . . . and nothing else. He perhaps might have even managed to convince himself, at least if necessary, that he had once seen that girl in one or another magazine and she impressed him and so was now a recurring impression . . . but again came a scraping noise from the neighbor's apartment, at first, as if it were just starting up again, seeking and testing out the most suitable places on the wall—there was scraping now at one end and a moment later at the other end of the bedroom wall, each time equally soft, as if tapping, testing, first in the upper right-hand corner just beneath the ceiling, then some five meters away in the lower left-hand corner near the floor, or the other way around, or here and there, and then up high again, then down below, in approximately the same spots as before, in other words, not blindly, not just anywhere, though without any discernible sequence—again and again, up above the wardrobe, to the left and right of the picture of the lonely sailboat in a storm, or down by his wife's nightstand, next to the ebony girl in the glass cabinet . . . Clearly, their previously peaceful, quiet neighbor, joined apparently by at least one other person, was now up to some madness, which slowly and intermittently gnawed away at Valent's nerves until it was nearly morning.

8

The fog had finally lifted, but it was too late to see the "mountain." And later in the morning his wife, returning from her "errands," learned that their neighbor, Mr. Kremavc, had died two days earlier in the hospital. This had been confirmed for her, she said, by the building manager, so she didn't want to hear another word about any scratching or pecking noises coming from their late neighbor's apartment. After that, Valent made up his mind to stop trying to convince her about these sounds and no longer force the issue, but then such a pecking started up next door that there could be no doubt whatsoever . . .

"Didn't you hear that?" he couldn't help asking. But the woman just looked around stupidly, shrugged her shoulders, shook her head no and said: "What?"

"Nothing." In a flash of anger he remembered her tranquilizers, and took comfort that he, too, was able to shrug his shoulders as if he couldn't care less and a moment later, as if totally indifferent, go into the bedroom. Even though he knew it would be hard for him to stay in the apartment. She came in after him. But he continued to change his clothes as if completely calm and, denying himself the pleasure of giving her some sort of look, set about tying his "office" necktie. Only then, as if to offer a courteous, good-hearted explanation, did he mumble something about how a person might occasionally imagine hearing something that turns out to be nothing in particular.

She didn't respond.

She only turned around and, as if offended for some reason, went back to the television in the living room.

He was glad to be left alone in the bedroom; glad, too, at the thought that he had maybe hit a nerve. A kind of inner laughter began to convulse and twist in his stomach, and it was joined by a, fortunately, controllable feeling that he had to do something right away, anything; that he was holding something big and round in his hands and it kept trying to roll away and needed to be restrained; and that there was also something big and round taking shape in his thoughts, and it seemed to him that, on top of everything, all this was making his eyes bulge out, at least a little. It was as if he were caught in a single, widely arcing wave. And then it passed. Safely. Even his heart remained calm. He only felt a little confused, a little worried by this feeling, which after all was out of the ordinary, and it made him wonder if in fact he had wanted to do something more than just confuse and upset his wife. And as for him changing his clothes and having "errands" to do in town, it was as if he had just now woken up and realized that he didn't actually intend to go anywhere and there was nothing he had to do in town—but all the same, he grabbed his black "office" briefcase and, as he was leaving, told his still pale and sulking wife (who had not even turned on the television), in a fairly conciliatory tone, that he would stop at the police station on the way. She said nothing. She didn't understand. But still he felt it was good and right that he had said this to her; it made him feel easier. And later, as he went along the street in his "office" clothes with his "office" briefcase among the people driving and walking past, he pretended to be a business-man in a hurry with thoughts only of business behind his serious frown, who had to get to where he was going without delay because as everyone knows time is money and the concerns that occupy a businessman's thoughts, a businessman's briefcase, are not to be sneered at. He held his head up and his briefcase a little away from himself, taking care that it did not bump against his leg, and every-thing had to be completely ordinary, customary, a little gruff, a little haughty; he might be going to the bank to review his accounts or check the latest exchange rates and such, or he might be going to the head office of the pensioners' meal service, and then on to the insurance company or the stock exchange—but for some reason it wasn't working for him now . . . In fact, he regretted having left the apartment, and that once again, as if caught in a kind of grip, he had to feign all this nonsense about the "office" look and the "office" briefcase, this hurrying, as if something were hanging over him, watching every second for any possible mistake in his stride or his demeanor or his thoughts, and this made his head ache with tension and uncertainty and every so often his heart seemed to skip a beat. This time he must definitely not go to a café. It was a kind of interdiction. And he definitely had to stop, if only for a moment, at the window of a jewelry store he'd noticed and try to see if the opals would jump out at him at his first glance.

He did not succeed—that is, not with his first glance.

This was perhaps why he then went into the perfume store; in fact, he was not entirely sure why, as he stood in front of the gently smiling saleswoman in full makeup behind the counter, nor as he managed to say in a fairly normal, casual voice: "Shalimar, please."

Then he shot a glance toward the door.

As if he had left somebody waiting outside on the sidewalk and was afraid this person might be coming in behind him that very second.

The saleswoman, with obviously practiced flirtatiousness, reached up to one of the higher shelves, and as she did so, her flimsy baby-blue dress rose high up her legs, exposing her ample, beautifully curved thighs.

He enjoyed the view. He also appreciated how she pressed her thighs together like a good girl as she stretched toward the shelf.

But the pressure in his head wouldn't let up. It was as though, even in the distractingly charming way she pressed her thighs together, there was something significant, something suspenseful.

"No need to wrap it up," he said quickly, stopping her as she reached for wrapping paper and ribbon. Then, maybe a little too hastily, he grabbed the perfume and, as if afraid of someone, quickly stashed it away in his briefcase. Only then did he pay and finally smile, with a wink and a nod trying to reassure the perhaps somewhat bewildered saleswoman that there was no problem. That he was satisfied with his purchase. And was going to leave now. And that her lovely, gentle little smile, which she once more endeavored to display, would be a pleasing farewell.

When he was back on the street that weird laughter, which definitely was not any sort of happiness, started coiling in his stomach again. It was as if some devil inside him was determined to burst out laughing at the most inappropriate moments and the most inappropriate things. While the Shalimar in his briefcase did indeed cause a certain degree of anxiety, he now felt a strange pleasure when he recalled how those ladies at the Little Paradise had uttered the word *phantom*; but at the same time, too, it all signified the ache now fermenting in his head again . . . Most of the people on the street were, just as on any other day, just like always, walking singly, silently, eyes to the ground; even clustered at streetcar stops or standing crammed together in the streetcar, they were the same: silent, each in his own world; only occasionally would someone in a couple or small group say anything or quarrel or even joke. Mainly, it was only the young people—and there weren't many of them—who still attempted to display a certain casualness, a certain nonchalance; the majority seemed to be under a spell, with eyes cast down or past one another; and the strumming or tooting of the occasional busker, in front of this or that store, sounded like nothing more than annoying, disingenuous begging. And in his painfully, miserably fermented thoughts, it was as if—in all this jostling and rushing and begging and crowding, all this pretense, these throngs of people, going here and there and who knows where, seemingly lost, in clusters or alone, beneath garish store displays and shop signs, through the rigid stillness of defaced passageways, colonnades, and arcades, past windows and walls—there was a kind of ecstasy that seemed to flash too hotly across their faces, seemed to blaze too feverishly in their eyes. People averted their eyes as they passed each other, remaining always equally alien and other; they were probably also averting their thoughts, just as he averted his as he tried to be ordinarily important, and as he then, as was his custom, entered on a whim, it didn't matter where, a building displaying a law office placard, climbed the stairs to the office door, jotted down in his appointment book: "Pavel Sas, Law Offices" along with the specified hours for receiving clients, and then went back out to the street slowly and as if he had seen to yet another matter.

And so he collected them.

And so he jotted them down.

While it was true that such a pointless activity did not always calm his nerves, in any case, as he told himself and tried to believe, it was certainly useful to have such information about lawyers, about their hours, close at hand.

He most often did this when he was possessed by the feeling that, despite people's seeming indifference to him, he had caught someone's attention on this or that street—the right thing to do, he felt, was to act like a man with serious matters to attend to, and especially now, when people might be suspecting him, might be tailing him, when the Shalimar in his briefcase would undoubtedly reinforce their suspicions, and when, in short, he could barely keep from looking around, looking over his shoulder, like someone being pursued. So he did not hesitate when, a short time later, he found himself at a building with a lavish entryway on which he read, among a variety of other signs and silver-edged black graffiti, the words "Law Offices of Metod Kunstelj, J.D."

He walked right in. And paid little attention to the clean-shaven, bald-headed man in the vestibule, evidently the security guard, who had obviously just been chatting, quite freely and casually, with the cleaning woman, who was leaning over the railing of the staircase. The moment they saw him, they became serious. The man turned a cold steely gaze on Valent, who merely nodded to him slightly as he passed through the vestibule and, looking neither at him nor at the cleaning woman but somewhere in-between them, made his way toward the staircase.

"The law office isn't open, sir," the woman said, as if she wished to spare him a needless climb up steps that she had perhaps just washed.

He was shocked. For a brief moment he stood there as if he'd been found out. He looked at the cleaning woman with some confusion and a second later, already having regained some composure, and as if expecting an explanation, turned to the security guard, who met his eyes with a suspicious stare. But now Valent couldn't be thrown off balance. He acted as if he himself knew very well that the law office was closed, as if, indeed, he had firsthand knowledge of the fact. And so, primarily for the sake of maintaining a proper businesslike impression, he continued toward the stairs.

"Sir!" The guard's voice was firm and decisive. "I need to see some I.D., please." Valent froze in mid-step. His heart started racing. He felt the cleaning woman watching him intently from above. And the guard closing in on him as if ready to take all necessary measures . . .

"Security Officer Just," the man identified himself dryly, approaching from behind, and then, still from behind, thrust some sort of identification card in Valent's face. Valent turned around, as calmly as possible, even with a kind of imposing dignity in his bearing and expression, and retrieved his own identification card from the inside pocket of his jacket, all the while endeavoring to maintain an official-looking cool and searching gaze.

"Here you are," he said with complete disinterest, as if resigned to the procedure, and handed him the I.D.

"Valent Kosmina . . ." the man mumbled, looking at Valent quickly and with a practiced eye, as if making sure that the face matched the photograph; then suddenly raising his head, he asked him directly, with piercing eyes, if he intended to visit Mr. Kunstelj, the attorney.

Valent needed but a moment to collect himself, to figure out a way to avoid any possible trap the man might be setting for him.

"I'm looking for Mr. Kremavc," he said, as if he also had a specific letter of permission in his pocket. If need be, he could add that he was fulfilling the last wish of his neighbor, who had passed away just two days ago, but that he did not know exactly where . . . But now the security guard was looking up at the cleaning woman. Valent, too, turned around and looked at her, his knees and legs trembling at the thought that now, maybe, he had really gotten himself into a mess, which, however, ultimately couldn't be so very hopeless since no one could prove anything for sure.

"Fourth floor on the left," the woman said, loud and clear. So loud that it echoed. And Valent felt a little dizzy from the amazement, the surprise. Which he had to keep from showing. Which he had to conceal. And quickly. Before he looked back at the security guard . . . Still, what a relief. Even if it was bizarre. Hard to believe.

But now with a "thank you" the guard had returned his I.D. and clearly had no intention of escorting Valent to the fourth floor. He simply walked back toward the front door. And then, probably in connection with some business relating to the attorney Kunstelj, leaned against the wall once more.

Nevertheless, Valent's knees were still shaking as he walked past the cleaning woman, who now wasn't even looking at him, and they continued to shake as he reached the third floor, where he rested a moment and tried to breathe out the pain in his chest; and then he had to climb yet another flight of stairs, for he was sure the two people down below were listening to his footsteps. It was only on the fourth floor, after he had calmed down somewhat, that he tried to work out what he would say to this Kremavc person, but he soon took comfort in the thought that in any case this man should be at least mildly interested in the chance of getting an entirely unforeseen inheritance from a possible relative.

Only very meager light, from a narrow window right next to the ceiling, penetrated the cramped and airless corridor of the fourth floor. At the top of the stairs there was a wide, useless alcove cluttered with overflowing cardboard boxes and other assorted junk. Here and there, wooden planks creaked beneath his steps. Neither of the two light switches in the left or right corridors was working, so he had to wait for his eyes to adjust to the dimness before he was able to read, and then only by getting very close, the names above the peepholes on the few doors that had nameplates. But the name Kremavc was not among them. Nor could he find the name anywhere in the corridor to the right of the staircase.

Unlike the floors below, this one had apparently never been renovated and the apartments there seemed deserted, with a lifeless silence hanging in the air.

Still, for the security guard's sake, he knocked on a door that was already slightly ajar, and to his great surprise heard someone rustling in the apartment.

Light, shuffling footsteps were approaching. The hook was lifted and the door opened a little wider. And between the doorjamb and the door, now opened just wide enough for a head to peek through, he saw an appealing face . . . a young girl, not much more than a child, with straight, silky black hair, was looking directly into his eyes with an expression of deep and seemingly innocent trust, and just continued to look at him like that, through the half-open door, with her soft, azure eyes, and she was clearly not the least bit embarrassed in front of a stranger.

"Who do you belong to?" In fact it was Valent who had to suppress, to swallow his own embarrassment. "Is your papa at home?"

She merely smiled and kept looking at him intently.

"What about your mama?"

He thought he recognized those soft azure eyes. Like they were saying something familiar. Reminding him of something. "I'm looking for Mr. Kremavc. Do you know a Mr. Kremavc?" He tried to stay calm, although it was difficult, although he no longer dared look directly into those azure eyes, and he really had no idea what he should do now, eye to eye with this girl, who clearly did not want to answer any questions, who thought it right, even amusing, to just look at him wordlessly and smile. The thought that he should not remain alone with this girl for too long was making him impatient. So he knocked on the door much harder, right above her head, and in a very loud voice asked through the opening if anyone was at home.

No reply came from within the apartment.

Not even a sound.

The girl, somewhat more serious now, was watching him with her deep-set eyes. She was not afraid. In fact, she seemed to be expecting something; beneath her mask of innocent trust she seemed to be hoping for some little token at least, perhaps a sweet, a piece of candy. And so, embarrassed and confused, and also fearing that he had already spent too much time alone with her, he opened his briefcase, where, after rummaging through the old newspapers and magazines, advertising brochures, insurance notices, bank statements, and his appointment book, he found nothing suitable . . .

"Why, you're quite a grown-up young lady, aren't you?" He smiled at her. She nodded. And gave him an adorably mischievous, self-satisfied smile. "And for such a pretty young lady," he continued, looking through his briefcase, "I just might have something here . . ." He now regretted opening the briefcase, regretted looking through it, since he should have known he did not have anything suitable for her. And now there he was in this awkward, stupid situation, as if unmasked. "Well, here's something. See?" He took out the Shalimar. The girl's smile spread into a great big grin.

He had never wanted, never intended, to give her something so unsuitable, something that he even felt was improper—he reproached himself as he hurried down the stairs, and wanted to turn around and go back—but it could have been even more awkward . . . If only he had said, this is for Mama, that she should give it to her mama . . . but as he was going down the stairs, right away, as soon as he reached the third floor, it was all affecting him differently, surprisingly differently; the security guard and cleaning woman had, it was true, thrown him off balance earlier; he had not, it was true, been paying proper attention to things, but the impression he presented would have to be, nevertheless, approximately the same as before . . . and on the second floor, to the right and the left, heavy chandeliers hung from the vaulted ceiling, light-colored marble wall panels gleamed above the mosaic tiles on the floor, and a new, luxuriously soft runner, which extended from the stairs all the way across the marble lobby to the front door, glowed with the colors of dawn . . .

The security guard and cleaning woman were no longer there.

9

He was tempted to confide in his wife. But he was gripped, paralyzed, by the miserable fear that he would just make a fool of himself, humiliate himself, and anyway, she would be neither able nor willing to understand. So all through lunch and the long afternoon, he kept his thoughts to himself, mulling things over and feeling lost, as if stuck in some horrible sticky ooze in which nothing was certain, nothing giving him comfort, while his nervously talkative wife prattled on and on, getting herself all worked up over one thing or another. There was a moment when he just wanted to ram his fist down her mouth, right out of the blue, and howl at her that this was no ordinary authority . . . and it was essential to be quiet.

That same idea had seized his heart. It lay there like a chilling shadow cast by a dark and swollen cloud. It pressed down on him, making his forehead bead with sweat and stopping his breath, as if he were terrified of the lightning it contained.

She noticed nothing. She was rambling on about some TV show or something, about someone who had nicely told, nicely advised the police commander, the captain, that an apartment like that should be protected, sealed off, since that's the proper thing to do, since we were none of us born yesterday and property is, after all, worth something.

He should enlighten her, should tell her that there was much more going on, that the commander only appeared to be a commander, and the captain, too, only appeared to be a captain, and that the whole thing, with all these appearances, was nothing but a fraud. But he knew there would be no point that somewhere, who knows when, they had both gotten lost. She was too far away. Too much that was alien had come between them, too many of these mundane truths that only seemed to be true, in the midst of which maybe they would never find each other again. And probably never find themselves. And the whole thing seemed as if a shadow had silently, stealthily spread across their souls . . . She was still talking, as if afraid of silence. Among other things, she said that "Mr." Mario had telephoned. That he wanted something from him, from Valent, and had said it was urgent. Valent made no reply when she asked him what business he might possibly have with "Mr." Mario. And just kept on looking at the puffs of steam and the purplish haze hanging over the city, just kept on thinking his thoughts, which glowed but dimly, as if trapped in some sticky ooze, and only occasionally attained a little clarity, though perhaps it was nothing but a hallucination. It was impossible to verify anything. Nothing could be proved. He would like to go back and see how that little girl was doing . . . but this could be exactly what they expected, since they probably knew that he was tormented by uncertainty, which made any thought he might have seem illogical, and therefore idiotic, senseless, and pointless.

His wife had stopped talking at last. As if she'd simply run out of voice . . . but she didn't leave the bedroom. Valent was still trying, nevertheless, to direct his thoughts toward the puffs of steam and all those hundreds of cattle needed every day for the city's daily meals, but these thoughts couldn't drown out the muffled, protracted scraping along the wall, as if someone in the Kremavc apartment was quietly, and very persistently, drawing a line. He felt a slight quivering in his stomach or somewhere thereabouts. Something was also happening with his lips and facial expression, all of which had to be coaxed into a more or less convincing display of indifference.

"It's all nonsense, Olga," he said, shaking his head, as if he mainly wanted to reassure her. He also tried to lower his voice somewhat, to make it soothing and soft. He walked over to the wall. And after listening intently a few moments, again shook his head. And shrugged. And as if he merely thought he might have heard something, as if momentarily uncertain because of some rustling overhead, he also looked at the ceiling. Actually, it seemed to him that the best thing would be to speak up, as if to instruct her and defend his own position in the house, to remind his wife, in a pointedly raised voice, that he very much regretted her inability to stand by his side as a wife should, by which he meant that there was nothing they could both believe in, and that a solution, even if one believed in such a thing, simply did not exist . . . Of course, it could still inspire sufficient courage so a person did not lose his dignity when, for instance, people suspected him of murder, that is to say, of one of the many murders that undoubtedly happen every day and go on happening and that, like the days themselves, are lost in oblivion. He would also like to tell her about the Shalimar and the little girl, and to stress the possibility that, for now, they might just be tailing him, observing him through this or that wall, which very likely meant they might come for him at any moment. They would have probably already done so, of course, if they did not have different purposes in mind. Different purposes!—he would say emphatically—different purposes!—maybe even raising his index finger to underscore the point. She might only look at him. Might only be amazed at him. And maybe she would finally understand that he was not just anybody, that is, not just one of her soap-opera characters, and the main thing was that he knew what it meant that they had not yet taken him away. Ah, these purposes!—he'd repeat, with suitable emphasis—these purposes, my dear! That's what this is all about—this scratching on the wall, this perfumed letter and Mario, and certainly the captain too, and many such captains, many such Marios, and other people too, and other things we don't need to ask about right now—it's all part of these purposes. Of course, if he were to raise his voice like that, and say all that, it would only make it worse. So for her sake, for her own good, it was better to say nothing. And she'd probably not believe it anyway, even if in the very early morning he were to show her the "mountain."

"And that's also a problem," he said, a little carried away.

She was looking at him as if something in his face was starting to make her afraid.

"That is to say"—he was getting confused—"a problem, yes, I'd say it's a problem if you don't believe me."

Obviously she didn't understand.

And that did not even seem important to him.

"You're strange," she could barely get the words out.

"We're all strange, Olga . . ."

"Valent!"

"Yes, that's what I think."

"Something's not right with you, mister."

"Heh, heh, heh." He opened his mouth a little more than he needed to. And flashed her his teeth. And looked up at the ceiling. And then back at her. And of course he would have done it again, over and over, but she stormed out of the bedroom as if stung in the backside.

"You'll hear the sounds too, yes you will! Heh, heh! Why shouldn't you?" he muttered to himself in a kind of jeer, then went back to the window and thought how she would be reaching for her strongest tranquilizers about now. And how all those herds of cattle were disappearing into the city's gullet every day, and how that thought wouldn't get anyone anywhere.

"That's true," he agreed, half-aloud. "It won't get anyone anywhere . . . because we are all trapped. Heh, heh. Because you are trapped too, Olga!" He said it loud enough for her to hear him, and then to himself alone: "And because they are trapped too."

"You have a telephone call." He had not heard her come back into the bedroom. He thought she must have taken an extra dose of tranquilizers; she looked contrite and walked and talked as if in the presence of a corpse. When he did not immediately turn away from the window, she mumbled something about him being deaf, and of course she did not understand that he couldn't care less about the telephone and that whoever it was who wanted something from him could just wait a minute. He did not move until she again, much louder, reminded him that he had a phone call; then he went to the phone and said, slowly, in a low drawl, "Hello." As soon as he heard the voice of "Mr." Mario, his heart sank. "Kosmina?!" The man had the gall to address him in this impudent way. It sounded like a warning. "Tonight, at 12:37, be in Gustav Kremavc's apartment." And that was all. Just like that. Without so much as a by-your-leave. 12:37 . . . after which this so-called "gentleman" simply hung up. Just like that, out of the blue. No explanation. No anything. And now his wife was standing in the bedroom doorway, watching as he tried to make sense of the dead air on the other end of the line and in frustration fairly slammed down the receiver.

"What'd she want?" she asked, demanding an explanation, the resolve in her voice concealed but adamant, as if the phone call concerned her too, or was even mainly about her.

"What do you mean, 'she'? That was . . ." He didn't understand. And looked away, embarrassed. And actually did not know what to say.

"Who was that little brat of a girl, Valent?" Obviously, she had not mistaken his embarrassment. And he couldn't say he was just pretending . . . but if he tried to explain it by telling her that maybe some little girl had made the phone call but that it was undoubtedly "Mr." Mario who then got on the line and continued the conversation, there would still be the difficult question of what it was, in fact, that this Mario person all of a sudden wanted.

"This 'gentleman' you like so much," he started to explain, as if he'd just had enough, "This Mario, or whatever he's called . . . he's looking for a new job"—he'd come up with something now—"and he's been pestering me to put in a good word for him somewhere." He tried to indicate to her, with both his voice and eyes, that at least as far as he was concerned, this conversation was over. But that only worked for a second, during which he heard a line being scratched across the wall.

"The little brat who called wanted to talk to you herself," she continued, not taking her eyes off him. She spoke as if she didn't want the neighbors to hear, but at the same time, the obvious tension in her voice told him she wouldn't put up with any of his games.

"But it was just Mario . . ." He tried to make a joke of it all the same, as if regretting that the "little brat of a girl" hadn't been more persistent.

"Oh really?" she said, with an even icier stare. "Mr. Mario is certainly not looking for any job."

He just shrugged his shoulders as if he didn't even think it worth joking about.

10

His thoughts were like a heavy burden that had piled up from who knows where. They came one after another, all in a tangle, in bits and pieces, or stretched into some miserable, unrecognizable, incomprehensible mass, and for the most part they were all just useless. Barren. In fact, they were commonplace, everyday thoughts, the kind everyone is familiar with, secondhand, threadbare, many already discarded, and none of them got him anywhere or gave him any answers. Mainly, all this stuff in his head just made him feel restless, with a nightmarish feeling of being in a hurry, like flashes and sparks crackling above an unseen fire someone kept poking at, that flare up and die down and mean absolutely nothing, nothing you could grasp or understand, since it was simply impossible for a person to find his way under such circumstances, since life and the city and everything else seemed both cheap and harrowing at the same time, since he didn't know how or with what or to what end he might make sense of anything, since all of it was making him tremble, making him wish it would just be over, one way or another. He had the feeling that all of it—bit by bit and at times distorted beyond recognition, from the street to the buildings to the people—was taking him over, all this rushing about, all these sounds from the television set, all this pointlessness, insignificance, worthlessness, which nevertheless demanded its daily meal every single day; all these appearances and guises, which were in fact forms of despair and bewilderment and confusion; and meanwhile maybe someone jumps or falls or screams, and of course it hardly mattered if one or another person died, if one or another person missed somebody or killed somebody, since all the while on television they just kept on doing what they do and no one was the wiser, neither here nor there nor anywhere. At that point, perhaps, it hardly mattered if you were this or that thing, if for instance you were a goat, or maybe an ant; it hardly mattered if you believed this thing or that thing or didn't believe it; what was important was that the daily meal was served and that nothing got muddled, that for instance all the cars and streetcars and trains didn't collide in one big pile-up, and that everything somehow seemed to run smoothly, so your wife could take her daily dose of tranquilizers and watch the different actors on television chase each other, cheat on each other, stab each other, or discuss healthy and unhealthy diets and diet supplements, which were part of the whole thing and had a positive influence on one's sense of well-being. The whole thing, yes. And at the same time you begin to suspect that you are, in a little way, part of the whole thing and that in fact there is nothing else. Fine, you tell yourself, the names will stay, but you also know that they are—or rather, will be later—increasingly redundant from day to day. And the whole thing is saturated with sounds, rumbling and vibrating, and meanwhile the evening passes slowly . . . and that line being scraped across the wall of the Kremavc apartment seems at some point to have stopped, and now there are only muffled, furtive rustling noises coming from over there, which catch your attention every so often through the sounds of the TV.

It was after eleven. His wife had fallen asleep . . . But Valent still had no idea what to do; he just kept moving about, changing his seat and pacing the apartment, stopping in front of the window and, again and again, through his own reflected outline in the glass, letting his gaze wander across the array of lights in the eastern districts, and he didn't know what he should actually do with all these thoughts. He was sorry he had not simply gone to Brežine, where, with a glass of burgundy and a well-stoked pipe, things might not seem quite so strange and forced, where he might have been able to simply forget about that "little brat of a girl" and "Mr." Mario, too . . . now it was too late—somebody, apparently, was already there waiting for him in his deceased neighbor's apartment . . . He tamped his pipe and lit it, then tried to settle his nerves in that slightly vague feeling of elation, of losing himself in the smoke, which was usually so agreeable . . . but now there was only a burning in his mouth, as if he had scorched it . . . and the saliva that gathered there was insipid and watery, was really just spittle, and he had to keep swallowing it with a feeling of revulsion.

Then his wife woke with a jolt, and in a kind of distracted bewilderment, sat up on the couch. She looked here and there . . . and clearly did not know what she was looking at or why, and for a brief moment her eyes rested on him, but then, as if he were not it—that is, not what she wanted, nothing special—she simply stood up and went into the bedroom. Just like that, without a word . . . It must be the drugs, he thought; she was more or less always stoned, and the two of them had become strangers . . . and he would just let them wait, whoever it was in Kremavc's apartment, if he went at all, of course, if he paid them any mind at all . . . and maybe whatever was about to happen had already been decided, who knows how or why, and all other possibilities were in fact just a cover . . . while people kept pushing and shoving, as if by some divinely spiteful decree, and they couldn't care less about all these names (who knows whose? who knows what kind?) that day in, day out, evaporate into oblivion like steam. But he had no idea what it was all about . . . or what this pain was, pressing in his chest.

He poured himself a glass of cognac and drank it.

It didn't help.

Nor did a second glass later. On the television, people were still chasing each other and beating each other up . . . His mouth still tasted watery, insipid—and now a certain doubt, a certain suspicion, was aroused . . . he was, after all, well aware of the fact that there was no one he could trust, no one who'd stand by his side in his present situation. His two sons would tell him some nonsense about how he was imagining it all and should just try to get some rest. There was no point in turning to the building manager or the police. After all, no matter whom he phoned, whoever was in the Kremavc apartment would hear him and of course have time to hide or slip away.

A little before twelve thirty he turned off the TV, shook out his pipe, and listened intently. There was only silence . . . from down below a muffled hum stretched across the city. Everyone in the apartment tower was probably already asleep. He couldn't even hear his wife's breathing. There was a ringing in his ears, it was true, and every so often his heart seemed to founder a bit and he had to control his breathing . . . but not the slightest sign of life could be heard from the Kremavc place. He even went up to the wall and pressed his ear against it. Nothing was moving. There wasn't the smallest sound. So the dead are all silence, he thought, and this hidden terror lying dormant in man is nonsense. And all that stuff about the Kremavc apartment was just a bad joke meant to confuse him and rob him of sleep. Which of course he wouldn't allow. Would definitely not let happen. First, he would go to bed. And then, maybe he would try to make himself believe in coincidence, that is to say, in the zero at the end of the equation, that is, in the zero on the right and left sides of the equal sign, and that all this stuff piling up everywhere from every side was nothing but a cover for nothingness, zero-ness.

So he had made up his mind . . .

But when he came out of the bathroom and turned off the lights, the telephone rang.

Long, horrible, sharp, it cut into the silence . . . but at the same time seemed somehow far away. Mainly afraid that the ringing might wake his wife, but also because of this weirdly annoying faraway sound in the ring, he ran into the front hall and simply unplugged the phone. And in the same moment, without clearly thinking about it, as if absolutely sure he'd find someone lurking outside, he unlocked the door and peered into the hallway.

There was only dense and silent darkness.

Nevertheless, though already in his pajamas, he stepped over to the Kremavc apartment and, without hesitating, knocked firmly and resolutely on the door. But the door, which must not have been fully shut, simply yielded to his knock, simply opened a little, which he hadn't at all expected; but even so, he managed to control his nerves, at least enough to call out, in a fairly strong, low voice and with apparent self-assurance, through the partially opened door into the dark, hollow silence: "Good evening."

No one replied.

He thought he smelled the sweet scent of Shalimar. But the next moment he was not entirely sure.

He called out a second time.

"Is anyone there?" he added after a pause.

It occurred to him that he should not go in there alone, that is, not without witnesses; that it could all be a trap they were trying to lure him into so they could then accuse him of robbery, or burglary, or something worse.

"It's . . . Kosmina here," he said in a much lower voice, standing in the doorway, just to be sure all the same . . . Then listening intently, he waited a little. Finally, after some time had gone by, he pressed the doorbell. Which didn't work. It had never occurred to him before that these meal-service agencies might be just a front, and that their so-called delivery people, who came into daily contact with elderly pensioners, knew precisely what was going on with every one of their clients. But now, he was almost convinced that whenever the opportunity presented itself, whenever one of their (ideally) solitary subscribers died, they would just come right into his apartment, maybe even in collusion with the building manager, and take whatever was most valuable, and then if need be, just to be on the safe side, they could use various tried and true ploys to cast suspicion on some naive neighbor . . . It definitely seemed the right decision not to enter the Kremavc apartment. He had not taken the bait. After all, it would be hard to explain later what he had been looking for in the middle of the night in his late neighbor's unlocked apartment. The best thing, he thought, would be to recruit some other neighbor as a witness and then go tell the building manager. But unfortunately, he did not have many close, or even particularly friendly, contacts with any of his neighbors. But that wasn't important now. So he switched on the hallway light and went to the nearest door, whose nameplate said "Vidic-Gross," and rang the doorbell. But he had to ring it twice, and then a third time, and was already losing patience when finally he heard a noise in the apartment and then a woman asking angrily who was out there and what did he want. Looking at him through the peephole, she asked if he had any idea what time it was, and then, in a louder voice, said that she would not allow this sort of—

"Madam," he interrupted her in his low Brežine drawl, "this is a serious matter." And asked straightaway if her husband was at home.

It was none of his business, she said.

"Please listen to me, madam," he nevertheless continued in a rather dignified, polite tone. "It looks as though somebody has broken into our neighbor's apartment and . . ." But she was obviously upset and wouldn't let him finish. What went on in someone else's apartment was none of her concern, all she wanted was some peace and quiet in the middle of the night . . .

"That's fine, madam," he broke in, trying to calm her down. "I just thought that if it were possible . . ."

"Why don't you call the police?" She didn't want to listen to him. "If you don't, I will, and right now, too," she said as if threatening him, and apparently, from somewhere in the apartment, had really gone to call the police.

That was fine with him. The police would have to be called anyway, eventually. But first, all the same, he wanted someone to be a witness. So skipping two or three doors without any nameplates, he went straight over to the apartment of the retired watchmaker named Marzi; he'd had coffee and a cognac with this fellow once and ever since they would always nod at each other in greeting. He rang the doorbell and at the same time called out for Mr. Marzi in a voice that was deliberately loud enough to be heard in another possibly occupied apartment on the floor.

This time he didn't have to wait long.

After looking through the peephole to see who it was, Mr. Marzi even opened the door.

"Oh my God, someone broke in, you say?" he said, alarmed and amazed after Valent told him briefly about Kremavc and the open door. Then he looked in the direction of the Kremavc apartment.

"I wonder if you would also take a look . . ."

"Yes, of course, of course." He was so upset he could hardly get the words out. And now Mrs. Marzi was at the door too. Pale and trying to arrange her rather disheveled hair, she at once wanted to know what was wrong.

"He says someone's broken into the Kremavc apartment," her husband explained in a hushed and somewhat confessional tone. Mrs.

Marzi immediately shot a glance at Kremavc's door and then, with a rather stern and judging look, gave Valent a good once-over.

"A lady in another apartment," Valent looked down the hallway, "Mrs. Vidic-Gross, has probably already called the police."

"Oh dear God!" Marzi was still shaking his head anxiously and looking around. Meanwhile, his wife, her arms folded over her chest, was eyeing Valent as if she had her reservations.

"Even this morning I heard someone walking around in there, scratching on the wall . . ."

"Really?" Marzi looked at him pointedly, his eyes highlighted by his gleaming bald head, which had just a bit of hair above the ears.

"Oletič should be told, too . . ."

"Oh, well, that Oletič fellow . . ." Marzi said dismissively of the building manager, though in a hesitant, muffled voice.

"And again this evening I heard a kind of shuffling sound . . ."

"So someone must have broken in," Marzi volunteered the obvious conclusion and once more looked over at the Kremavc place. But by now Mrs. Marzi was already on her way down the hall, and the other two followed.

Valent wondered a moment whether he should try to persuade the Marzis to go in with him, all three together, and look around the apartment, but then he decided it would be best if the suggestion came from them.

But the door to the Kremavc apartment was completely shut.

Locked. As Mrs. Marzi discovered.

Valent needed to make sure for himself nevertheless, and so pressed down hard on the door handle—since, really, this was incredible, and quite aggravating too, of course; it put him in a very awkward position, as the three of them exchanged looks and he did all he could to maintain the composure of a self-assured and thoroughly respectable man.

"Yes, it seems that . . ."—Marzi had bent down to the keyhole and was examining it from every angle—"it doesn't really look as if . . . No, I wouldn't say the lock has been tampered with."

Valent did his best not to appear ridiculous as he felt Mrs. Marzi's eyes on him, but he had no idea what to think or say that might help even a little.

Marzi looked up from the keyhole and, still looking at it, shrugged.

"It was definitely open earlier," Valent insisted. But now, even to himself, he seemed less than convincing and not at all Brežine-like. Mrs. Marzi was watching him from the corner of her eye.

"If it *had* been broken into . . ." Marzi said, still shaking his head and looking at the keyhole.

"Wait a second," Valent whispered—he'd figured it out now—and placed a hand meaningfully on Marzi's shoulder. "They're probably still in there."

Marzi looked at Valent, then at his wife. She evidently had her doubts about Valent's hypothesis.

"You think they locked themselves inside?" Marzi, too, seemed doubtful now.

"Yes, I do." He saw no need to conceal his disappointment at the rather insulting second thoughts they seemed to be having. It was true he hadn't checked before to see if the apartment had actually been broken into, and that was how he had described the situation to them—but he certainly didn't intend to go into any of this now. A little impatiently, as if wondering why it was taking the police so long to get there, he looked down the hall toward the elevator and a moment later, with a measure of proud disdain, looked straight into Mrs. Marzi's eyes. Which, at least, she appeared to take in stride. She even let out a yawn.

"Well then, so now . . ." Marzi sighed with a shrug, mainly out of consideration for Valent, it seemed, but obviously he had no idea what to say.

"We wait for the police to get here," Valent said in a low but determined voice.

"Yes, of course." Marzi was not entirely sure. But he clearly thought it best to keep his reservations to himself. In the meantime, Mrs. Marzi had stepped right up to the door and with a finger to her lips indicated to the two men that she thought she might have heard something. All three held their breath.

Quite a bit of time passed before Mrs. Marzi finally shook her head with a scowl, stepped back from the door, and said that she, for one, didn't believe there was anyone in there.

"What if we . . ." Marzi began again, but didn't finish.

"They're lying low," Valent whispered.

Again, the three of them were silent. And as if embarrassed, they avoided each other's eyes. Then all of them in unison turned to look at the elevator as it started to rumble. But apparently it was stopping on one of the lower floors.

And then, a while later, it went up to a higher floor.

"The door *was* open," Valent broke the silence in a low, confidential voice, having sensed that the Marzis lacked the will to keep this hallway vigil up for long. "Then I went over to *that* apartment"—he nodded toward the Vidic-Gross place—"but I never once let this door out of my sight." That wasn't entirely true, since Mrs. Vidic-Gross's foul mood had caused him to forget, briefly, about the open door, and then later, while he was going down the hallway—that is, to the Marzis'—he didn't exactly keep his eye on the Kremavc apartment the whole time. But he was sure he would have heard something if someone had slipped out of the apartment in the meantime, especially if they had locked the door behind them. Still, the stairs and the elevator were not very far away, just seven or eight steps at most. But he really saw no reason to doubt his supposition that the door had been locked from the inside. Of course, his suspicions fell on "Mr." Mario and, more and more, on the building manager too. But for now he did not want to mention any of this.

When after a really unconscionable length of time the police had still not appeared, he realized that Mrs. Vidic-Gross had never telephoned them at all. So he suggested that perhaps Mrs. Marzi should phone the police and, naturally, demand an explanation for why they were taking so long to get here.

But she replied that it would be better for Valent to call them himself since he could more easily describe what had happened; she wouldn't know what to say, after all, and anyway, as far as she was concerned, the best thing would be for them all just to go back to bed.

But she stayed there all the same, though it seemed, at least on the surface, that she wasn't happy about it.

"I had thought it might be better if your husband and I stayed here by the door," Valent tried to explain amicably. "Who knows, they might try to make a run for it."

"Oh, for God's sake!" She no longer saw any need for whispering. "There's no one in there!"

"What about Oletič?" Now Marzi was trying to be amicable.

"I think," Valent whispered, leaning toward him and pointing his thumb at the door, "that it's Oletič who's in there."

This made an impression on Marzi, or at least seemed to. He even nodded as if he understood and agreed. But the next moment he looked again at his wife, and in their quick exchange of glances Valent detected something like a hint of mockery. This stung him, but it also made him more determined to make that telephone call. To prove them wrong and wipe those mocking looks off their faces. And so without saying another word, but inwardly fuming, he hurried back to his own apartment with long and decisive steps.

But on entering the front hall, out of the corner of his eye he caught a glimpse of the girl, just as she was slipping off into the living room.

He was stunned; for a second he even thought he was going to faint . . .

He remembered the appointment, of course, and the letter, this "seal upon your heart," and thought that maybe it was not all a prank. The luxuriant fragrance of a heady sweet perfume still lingered in the front hall.

His heart, as if suddenly squeezed, seized up a few times. So he had to lean against the wall.

Thoughts crowded in on him all at once. The girl was definitely somehow here, but . . . he didn't understand . . . there was too much he had to grasp, all of it at once and fast, and who knows what he had to figure out . . . the girl being here was somehow annoying, an unpleasant surprise . . . still, he had no wish to betray her, or to wake up his wife . . . and without thinking it through, without really knowing why, he said, "Hello!" as if talking on the telephone, although not picking up the receiver but directing his voice toward the front door . . . "The door was unlocked. It was open, yes . . ." he continued. "Mr. Kremavc's apartment, the one who just died . . . yes, yes, but someone's locked it now . . . yes, that same apartment . . . Tomorrow? What do you mean, tomorrow?! But really . . . None of our business? Why, of course it is! We're his neighbors, after all . . ." He was amazed at how easily it came to him and thought that, hidden somewhere in the living room, the little girl must be thanking him, must even be admiring him.

"I'll be back in a second," he whispered toward the living room, as if confiding something, after which he hurried back out, and the Marzis, even at a distance, were trying to tell from his face what was happening and how things stood.

Naturally, he feigned disappointment as he told them in a few words that the police were not coming, or rather, that they would be here but not until tomorrow and that this was supposedly no concern of even the closest neighbors.

The Marzis exchanged glances.

And just stood there unable to make a decision, as they all looked back at the door and down the hallway, and as Valent tried with difficulty to conceal his nervousness and trembling and impatience, his curiosity, in fact, which was also a kind of pull and lure, and he even found it hard to breathe as he started apologizing—indecisively, as it were, as if he didn't know what else to do—for disturbing them in the middle of the night, but now, given the views of the police, he didn't think it wise for them to take matters into their own hands.

The other two said nothing.

Marzi pursed his lips and shook his head. Mrs. Marzi, it seemed, was keeping her thoughts to herself; in any case, she offered no comment, or maybe just had nothing to add.

"What do you two think? I really don't know . . ." Valent said after a pause; he wanted to hear them say something.

"Hmm . . . I don't know . . ." Marzi muttered.

"I've said what I have to say." His wife shook her head as if in reproof. Valent didn't like the way she shook her head. But now he did not have the time, or the desire, to delve into it. He merely shrugged his shoulders to let them know they could do whatever they felt was best.

"Of course, we could still wait here." He tried to sound convincing. Naturally, he expected at least Mrs. Marzi to disagree. But she didn't. Instead, she asked if he had called the building manager too.

He shook his head.

"He thinks, you know . . . that Oletič might be in on it," Marzi stammered, whispering, to his wife.

"Well, I mean, I can't be sure . . ." Valent said evasively, as if mainly he didn't want to be held accountable. "A person can think one thing or another about such-and-such a matter, but if the police say—I mean, what do I know?—if they're not particularly interested, well, then . . . you mind your own business and then something happens and suddenly you find yourself in the middle of it all."

"You look a little pale, Mr. Kosmina," was Mrs. Marzi's only comment. And Valent felt a slightly stronger tightening in his chest.

Such remarks alarmed him. But still he managed to collect himself enough to say something about how late it was, and how none of them was getting any younger, and so on, and even attempted a smile, but he wasn't very successful. Now Marzi, too, was eyeing him with a rather concerned and somewhat pitying look; he obviously agreed with his wife's assessment.

"I wonder what was wrong with him—Mr. Kremavc, I mean," Mrs. Marzi continued, as if that could have something to do with Valent's paleness. They both wondered.

"I really don't know," Valent said, with a note of frustration in his voice. "After all, one doesn't get involved in other people's affairs, and we actually hardly ever saw each other. And now this happens. I don't know if it makes any sense . . ." Apparently they didn't know either. So Valent just turned around and took a few steps toward his apartment, and then, as if remembering something, turned back to them, shrugged his shoulders, and muttered, as if to himself, that it really made no sense at all. He was getting more and more impatient. He was even afraid someone else might join the three of them there in the hallway and then it would all drag on until morning, which of course would mean that the girl wouldn't be able to leave his apartment without being seen. His wife, of course, would raise hell and a half. And then everyone would know that he had never called the police and who knows what else. There would certainly be trouble, there would certainly be unpleasantness, and to top it off, the little girl would never forgive him.

"Know what? I, for one, am going to bed," he finally told them. He knew the Marzis would look at him strangely, would think all sorts of things . . . "I'm not feeling so well," he added, and with a worried look, shook his head. Then—as if he had done all that a worthy man could and must do, without paying any attention to their long silent stares, and sensing that he had not convinced them, that he had, even about his own behavior, almost certainly aroused their suspicions—he simply walked back to his apartment, shut the door, and locked it behind him.

11

But the girl was nowhere to be found. He looked everywhere she could have been hiding, even in the bedroom . . . In truth, he was a little relieved by the fact that she seemed to have simply vanished, relieved mainly because of his wife and all the aggravation that would have probably ensued. Still, it was far from true that he was happy about it, that he didn't also feel stupid and disappointed, played for a fool, and generally wretched over what was clearly a practical joke, but the sort of joke you can't easily come to terms with because it gnaws at you, because you're ashamed and angry, because in fact you're furious with yourself and simply don't know what to do or where to turn. At least three times he searched the entire apartment, even checking to see if the windows were shut—after all, a girl like that really isn't such a very tiny thing; confused, baffled, he sat down in his armchair, but then stood up again and looked around to see if anything was missing in the apartment. He simply could not believe there was any way she could have slipped into the hallway when, after all, the lights were on and he was standing out there with the Marzis, who had been facing his apartment the whole time. He considered going back out to them and confessing everything; he would ask them, that is, explain to them somehow, try to convince them somehow—true, it would be horrible and awkward; true, they would think all sorts of things, especially Mrs. Marzi of course . . . So there was nothing for him to do, then, but sit back down in the armchair where, after a while, on top of it all, he became bothered and upset by the idiotic thought that maybe the girl simply did not exist . . . of course he could take one of his wife's tranquilizers, maybe several—enough to discover whatever it was that a person discovered that way, if there was anything to be discovered. But it was this uncertainty that was the devil here, or the god, or both; it was a kind of curse, or force, that made you choose cognac instead, though after the first gulp you realized cognac wasn't the thing either, that is, it wasn't what you wanted, and that everything, all of it, was subject to something you didn't know and probably couldn't discover. A watery, slightly sour aftertaste remained in his mouth, even after he went to get a new bottle and downed a few gulps from it, yet nevertheless, he tried to feign (if only for his own benefit) something like contentment or certainty or whatever might calm his nerves . . . or what would suit, let's say, some sort of exclusive elite group or, for instance, Dr. Pavlovski, who somehow did exist, though maybe not completely and also not so that he could understand what it actually was that people called uncertainty and what you must of course hide if you want to be suitable, if you want to be known as somebody people are willing to look up to, listen to, and respect. Dr. Pavlovski, naturally, in such a situation—concerning the girl, that is—would proudly, dismissively refrain from comment, even if the little girl were to dance across the table in that little pink skirt she wore, even then he would insist . . .

"But I did see her, after all," he mumbled out loud, and shrugged.

"That is as certain as it is certain that I am sitting here, as it is certain that I will die," he raised his voice and tried to sound convincing, as if he really were sitting next to Dr. Pavlovski . . . who would probably just look at him dismissively.

"You, too, will die then." The very thought of this conceited, superior attitude infuriated Valent. "All of a sudden, without fail, mercilessly . . . And you will be dead with me, just like Kremavc is dead, and whoever else in all these damn buildings." And a moment later, for no particular reason, he threw his glass on the floor. And thought, this is what a man does in his own home with his own things if that's what he feels like doing.

"Now that's a fine argument," Dr. Pavlovski would nod, mocking him.

"That's just what I mean!" Valent almost yelled. "That's exactly what I mean!" His throat was choked up with rage, and the bottle found itself in his hand and, then, as if by its own volition, shattered on the floor.

He felt a stabbing pain in his heart, several times, as if from a sharp needle.

And then it abated.

And settled into a kind of misery . . . which fogged his eyes, which were fixed on the sour-smelling bottle shards, and fogged his thoughts that life was somehow like that and that was why his chest hurt, and that the whole thing was going nowhere except back to those sour-smelling shards of glass . . . even if a man was to burst into tears or hang himself or take a lot of sleeping pills so everything would go dark, or maybe radiant, so it would all pass, or maybe only really begin. To top it all off, he was also sorry he had so badly stained, nearly ruined, that rather good carpet, and that the spreading stain reeked of sourness . . . Fortunately, his wife was still asleep. But even if she woke up, he would probably just keep staring at that broken glass and at those thoughts, which were like tiny splinters among bigger shards, on which it was very possible to hurt yourself, to cut yourself. In fact, that possibility was mostly what they meant, almost nothing else. Who could put them back together into the meaning they once had . . . ? Love, too, was like that, it seemed to him: you couldn't put it back together again, not even when there's a little girl with soft azure eyes. All you have left is this awful, painful confusion, and maybe the possibility, out of courtesy and consideration for others, of cleaning up after yourself, since even if it's your own home and your own things you don't want to make a mess, you don't want to leave stains. No one, after all, is interested in whether your eyes have fogged over, or whether they sometimes seem filled with steam from the slaughterhouse chimneys, or whether there's a searing pain in the center of you, whether your life is like some fairy tale, whether, as in a dream, a black-haired little girl has come back from who knows where . . . and now silently approaches, on tiptoe, and with her index finger placed against her lips, which look eager to be kissed, she signals for you not to say a word. Because of your wife, probably . . . He wants to stretch out his hand, but it doesn't obey him, nor does his leg; and even his head is governed by some sort of insubordination, which is agonizing of course; and it's hard for him to keep turning his eyes up and to the side toward the girl, a problem she doesn't seem to notice at all and instead smiles at him with her lovely little mouth, with her flirtatiously restless azure eyes, as she steps right across the broken glass on the carpet barefoot and, from the waist down, below her little white silk blouse, is naked, and the nipples of her barely budding breasts protrude prettily beneath the silk, just a smidgen, and the childishly downy but already chocolate-colored little pout between her legs is mainly a kind of innocent beguilement . . . Of course, he is surprised, dismayed, and can't say what he would like to say; he only manages to stammer out his fear about the broken glass on the floor—but apparently there's no need, for she simply walks across the shards and smiles and doesn't seem to feel the glass splinters piercing the soles of her feet, doesn't even notice when a larger piece of glass slices her foot long and deep from heel to ankle; she only says, "Look, I'm wearing opals," and unbuttons the top of her blouse, leaning forward just enough to show him a necklace of black opals around her neck.

"What?" Valent mumbles.

"A necklace." She winks as if mainly pleased that she managed to surprise him a little.

He wants to say the necklace looks nice on her, but instead he has to gasp for air; he wants to ask if she is also wearing Shalimar, but he dreads the thought. Then, in fact, he does smell the heavy, sweet scent of Shalimar emanating from her. "I'm not feeling very well," he starts to say, although he knows that it's foolish to try to wriggle out of the situation—which he soon deciphers from the offended look on her little face—or show himself to be a weakling; her eyes, too, are colder now, glassy somehow, and the smile on that darling little mouth has somehow died away.

"Don't you want me here?" She sighs, as if hurt.

"Yes, I do!" He tries to make things right, but he's obviously all too confused. "It's not that I don't want you . . ." He cannot think of anything the least bit clever to say, anything that might, at least a little, correct the impression he's made. It's no use. So he just stops talking and turns his eyes away, not daring to look again at her nakedness. "It's just that the light is strange," he finally manages to add. "Red as wine . . ."

"Yes, red as wine," she echoes, as if absorbed in thought, and her soft whisper is again enticing. He can only look at her and listen, and maybe he only imagines her mentioning, in a very quiet whisper, something about a campfire dance, but he doesn't actually understand what she's talking about—and then she says: "Love is as strong as death." He's not entirely sure about this, either; also, the light isn't exactly red, but the stains are still on the carpet, and this is probably turning his thoughts red, probably turning her words red, as well as the scent of the Shalimar, so that the whole thing is like being in some temple with a freshly wounded, voluntary victim of sacrifice, and he too, without knowing how, has evidently sliced the sole of his foot and there's a splinter of glass lodged painfully in the wound. Of course, he'd look for it and pull it out, if only the blood weren't oozing from the deep, ugly wound, and if at that moment he hadn't been startled by his wife, who was standing there, pale and puffy-faced, staring at him transfixed—he had not heard her enter from the bedroom. She seemed to have a nervous tremor. She might very well have seen the girl, who was probably hiding—there were bloody footprints (maybe only his) leading to the tall section of the glass cabinet . . . which, perhaps, his wife was only pretending not to notice.

"Just look at yourself!" she said, scowling of course, as if about to be sick. "What in the world is wrong with you?! And this!"—she pointed with disgust at the bloody mess on the floor—"What in the world do you call this?!" He could have said, it's life; he could have said, it's not so important what you call something and now is not the time for all this soap-opera foolishness, but he thought it better to say nothing. It was obvious, after all, that she was still sedated. But maybe she could help him anyway.

"Look . . ." he said with a groan, pointing at the footprints that led to the cabinet. But she didn't understand. He should just be sure to clean it up, she muttered contemptuously from the bathroom door, adding something about shameful filth and that it made her want to vomit, after which she was already rummaging through the bottles and boxes of tranquilizers. He roused himself and hurried after her into the bathroom. And shut the door quickly behind him.

"What do you want?" she said gruffly, glaring at him.

"Nothing . . ." He instantly changed his mind and then just watched as she swallowed one or two or however many pills, her face rigidly bloated, and then put the water glass down firmly on the shelf above the sink, as if he were the reason she needed those tranquilizers. He tried to take her hand, but she pulled it away and, with enraged revulsion in her face, in her movements and in her step, rushed out of the bathroom. And slammed the door.

Then he sat there a while, right where he was . . . on the rim of the tub.

And thought about what his sons would say, and their wives, what they would whisper to each other . . . even if what had happened to that man in Brežine were to happen to him.

In the meantime, he heard his wife go into the bedroom, and he noticed how the apartment grew quiet again, lonely somehow; blood was dripping silently on the tile floor, and in spite of everything, there still burned in his heart the hope that the girl might, at any moment, once she was sure his wife had really fallen asleep, slip into the bathroom . . . His vision was still foggy and dizzy and ruddy; also, the thought that most murders and suicides happened in the bathroom was starting to frighten him; but the consoling idea that many other things happened in bathrooms too, and with far greater frequency, was beginning to merge—despite his misgivings and as if on its own accord—with newly-awakened expectations of warm closeness and soft surrender . . . it would certainly be nice to cup his palm a little over that warm chocolate-colored pout of hers and simply forget all about the opal necklace and everything else . . . which most probably—maybe even in connivance with "Mr." Mario, and with one of the Brežine inspectors to boot—was only their way of testing him.

He hastily cleaned himself up the best he could and bandaged his bleeding foot.

And having made up his mind to pull the girl out of the cabinet as quickly as possible and, despite everything, send her home, he left the bathroom.

Like a man in his own home. Like a man who knows his duty.

And he opened the cabinet . . . but there was no one inside. Even the bloody footprints had somehow disappeared.

Then he quickly looked in the kitchen.

And in the front hall.

The key was still in the door. But it was unlocked . . .

Doubt, suspicion, disappointment, anticipation—everything was getting tangled, one thing displacing another, as he once more searched and conjectured and tried to understand . . . He even looked in the bedroom under the bed, and in all the wardrobes, one after the other, in his wife's clothes, his own clothes, in the hamper, under this table and that one, behind the drying rack in the corner, but he could not accept that this was how things were . . . and through all that impatient poking about and moving around, his wife stayed sound asleep.

A pale light, meanwhile, had begun to show in the windows.

Brightness crept over the rooftops. The hum of the waking city was growing noticeably louder.

And Valent, finally, just stood there as if lost—and looked around, listening . . . everything around him was standing or sitting or hanging in its own silent motionlessness and that silent motionlessness made everything alien. Even the statuette of the too-young but nonetheless vain little girl in the glass cabinet looked alien, and the waves in the painting and the little boat were silent, and along with the chandelier and the little table and the armchairs, the sofa and the television set, expressed a kind of alien loneliness, a pathlessness, in the midst of which one is seized with despair.

"Shulamite!" he called softly; the name had come to him.

"Shulamite . . ." he repeated toward the cabinet. But from every corner there was still only, as if entirely, silence—there was not a single rustle or movement or the least indication of anyone's presence anywhere. Wherever he aimed his thoughts, they returned with emptiness, with a loneliness that ached and wrapped itself in timorous sorrow, into which he tried, as if for consolation, to summon her darling face and dreamlike azure eyes, her sweet whisper, and smooth, shoulder-length black hair, silky and shimmering . . . But the image, hazy and distant, eluded him, like a fading dream that you try in vain to capture and keep . . . when, indeed, it doesn't fade away completely; when, indeed, what remains of it is like what remains of the sea waves, a frozen picture on the wall, and at the same time you know that what remains is by no means enough to be any sort of consolation.

12

Above the eastern districts, a pale grayness curved into the still-darkish morning blue like a sprawling mass of mountain. A little closer, the puffs of steam from the slaughterhouse chimneys seemed almost white. In the windows of the apartment block settlements, whether nearer or more distant, a few lights were coming on above the shallow effulgence of the street. But through it all, everywhere around him, persisted the thought of Shulamite . . . who—for him at least, at least for now—had no other name; who couldn't have simply vanished, evaporated, faded away, and so disappeared into the zero at the end of the equation—or at the end of reason, perhaps . . . After all, he couldn't help wondering whether all the goings-on of this past night had been for real—or had he only dreamed them? Or maybe all of it had somehow just woven itself together, on its own, out of his thoughts, in the middle of which there was now a gaping hole and a yearning to possess her image . . .

Here and there in the grayness there were arcing crests and curving vales; there were rib-like protuberances falling in folds or jutting out into a kind of overhang, and one could imagine rocky hollows hidden within these bluffs and beneath one or another a stream or a mountain trail. It seemed, in fact, to be a real mountain wilderness, which at the first barely blushing trace of the waking dawn started glowing from inside, as it were, into a slightly purplish tinge. Isolated white puffs of steam hovered at the base, as if a part of those herds that had just become the daily meal were now returning, as the blue above the city, above the puffs of steam and the "mountain," grew brighter, and the crimson at the base of the vaulted mass lost its initial bluishness and turned into an ever more fiery orange. The puffs of steam, too, especially from the most distant chimneys, were acquiring more and more of a reddish tinge. And soon there appeared from behind the "mountain," now glowing in spots as if with spilt wine, the burning red ball of the sun, in all its silent dignity.

The "mountain" had, for today, said all it had to say.

And this might have indicated something positive, had it not been for the lingering uncertainty about Shulamite, about the memory of her, which filled him with fear. After all, the scratching sounds from the Kremavc apartment, the open door, and Shulamite herself—the same kind of thing could have also happened at that villa in Brežine, with the Shalimar, the opals, and the sliced neck . . . He found it impossible to be sure of anything. There were only vague apprehensions dumbly staring out at him . . . and high above, like a fiery spear across the blue of the sky, an airplane was making its way from the west.

When the sun had ascended into gleaming whiteness, there stretched across the city, across the chimneys and the horizon, as on every clear morning, a thin, stifling, grayish haze. Although one could still see through this haze, even to the most distant chimneys, the "mountain" was now an ever-fainter silhouette that would soon be only a mist subsiding in places along its edges into blue sky.

And then white clouds were strewn across the sky, and the city's hubbub was in full swing, and the newspaper was probably already waiting for him in the mailbox, but Valent just stood there peering out the window and couldn't decide whether he should, as he usually did, get dressed, and like any important businessman pressed for time, hurry down to get the newspaper. The Marzis were probably waiting for him, watching for him, although he would rather not think about them. He preferred instead to look, as if randomly, at one and then another spot in the east, and then, based on the faded colors of whichever of the various apartment towers his glance happened to fall upon, try to determine whether or not she would ever come back. In the same way, too, he tried to make guesses about the crime in Brežine, and would count how many times in a row, as he glanced back and forth, his eyes fell on a green tower or a yellow one, a brick-brown tower, or even a red-and-white one, a gray one or a bluish one . . . such random sequences could mean a lot—in fact, he had often read or heard or seen on television stories about various kinds of deranged people, insane criminals, memory lapses, delusions, phantoms, and they always scared him a little.

Physically, too, he felt fairly awful this morning. It was true of course that he had been up all night, and had had a bit too much cognac (which was now taking its toll), but still, the fatigue in his chest and arms and legs was greater now than it had ever been before under similar circumstances. It seemed to pass through him in waves. From time to time he would feel a painful tightening in the chest, and his vision would get dim or shaky, or he felt that his knees were about to give way, or that the floor had simply vanished beneath his feet. And then, he thought, he would probably fly, or . . . but maybe it wouldn't be like that at all, maybe it would only be the end, just like that, simple, and in its essence, complete—self-evident, as it were. No more uncertainty, no more questions, no more confusion or apprehensions or difficulties, just one eternal completeness, which would never end anywhere . . . and would never begin anywhere.

Although weak and shaky, he decided to clean the carpet. He had to pick up or vacuum the shards and splinters of glass and scrub out the stain. But the main thing was to forget, to put out of his thoughts, his fatigue and his heart, and then to wait, simply and thoughtlessly, for his daily meal.

In places it still smelled of Shalimar.

But he told himself that none of it made any sense, nor did many other things. And he just kept on cleaning. And did not look at his wife when she came in all cross from the bedroom.

"Just look at yourself, what you're doing," she grumbled before going into the bathroom and shutting the door behind her. And it seemed to him it was all always the same, somewhat stale and used up, the air too, and he would only make it worse if he opened a window. Maybe there would be some small relief for a little while if she turned the TV on this very minute, if someone on TV would be talking, or singing, or sighing, if for some reason or another they'd be beating each other up and killing each other—or all that at once—and if she too was mainly that, along with the apartment and apartment tower, and all the eastern districts, and all the puffs of steam . . . But instead she came in later and, more or less as in some soap opera, served the coffee and said she'd had a terrible dream. He could have asked her about it but he really was not in the mood to listen to her talk about her dreams and her troubles, and in fact he did not even want to be around her.

"There was someone lying on top of me," she started to tell him anyway, if only because there has to be conversation with morning coffee, since morning coffee is a form of sociability with a universally established etiquette that must therefore, if for no other reason, be followed.

"I think it was some sort of child, a little girl . . ." She let out a quick laugh that barely concealed her nervousness, as if one certainly had to laugh about such things. Then, as if changing her mind about what she wanted to say, she continued in an entirely different direction: "I always wanted to have a girl; so did you . . ." Valent was now listening more intently, and even felt a chill go through him, but his wife couldn't have noticed. "Maybe it wasn't a girl, after all . . . I don't know; it was all so silly." Obviously, she knew from the start she wouldn't tell him everything—that, as usual, she would only mention some detail out of politeness, and then, as if she thought it too trivial for him, would conclude her story with a sneer. She raised her cup to her mouth and took a small sip. As usual, her little finger extended unnaturally from the cup's little handle, and her eyes, too, shone with an affected pleasure in her coffee sipping, which always revolted him. Meanwhile, something about coincidences went through his mind, but it was too foggy and talking about it would require some effort, so instead he said he had to go out on errands, although this was not at all what he had been planning and it was quite bothersome, in fact, when this statement popped out of him on its own accord, as it were. He felt much too weak, much too tired, to do anything of the sort. But what was said was decisive, like some unquestionable obligation that couldn't be ignored.

In fact, she would often start some seemingly intimate conversation like this with him—always when they were having their morning coffee—and then, maybe offended by his unwillingness to play along, turn bitter and sarcastic. He knew this would happen now, too. And in the pit of his stomach he felt that shudder, that repugnance, which sometimes really did seem a little unfair, but he couldn't help but convey, if only through the barely visible trace of contempt in his seemingly attentive face, that in fact he was no longer interested in what she might ever have wanted for herself or in anything of the like. Even what he might once have wanted for himself was for him now merely bothersome and pointless. Even the idea of having a daughter. And all such things and other things and who knows what else of all that which never had come true and that rotted pointlessly away in his memory. And in fact it now seemed to him, more than not, that he had never really wanted a daughter at all, that others had at some point attributed this desire to him. And he simply had not denied it at the time. Or anytime later. He might even say that now, without any regard for his wife's poorly acted moans of disappointment which would surely follow.

Then she said the whole apartment stank and it was all really too much. The fact that he had tried to clean the carpet had of course escaped her notice. Nor did she show the least bit of interest in his injured foot or his headache or his heart pains. On the contrary, he knew she would not spare him, that she would make spiteful use of the opportunity and once again rub salt in whichever of his wounds was most painful—wounds that were, in one way or another, past healing. So before she started in on him about the ruined carpet and so forth, he might as well simply tell her straight out that he was aching for Shulamite and so really did not need any of her spitefulness or criticism. Her eyes would no doubt pop out of their sockets; she'd no doubt make some innocent-looking face; and she'd simply not understand that he was not and never would be any soap-opera León or Joe, nor was it possible to see in her some elegant lady from her serials.

But instead he got up from the table without a word and limped off to the bedroom. But at the thought that he might lie down, at least for a moment, he was seized by fear for his heart: that, he sensed, would only make it race, make it fluctuate all the more, and so despite everything he decided to get dressed and stay on his feet at least a little while longer. After all, he could go down and get the newspaper, or go to a nearby café and so distract himself, at least a little, and rid himself of this tension that was causing quivering and tightness in his chest and stomach, and also rid himself of the fear that this tension, this tightness, might suddenly become a needle-like stabbing in his heart.

He shut the window. And drew the curtains. And sat on the edge of the bed. And thought of the Marzis, who were probably waiting for the police to arrive and watching to see when he would leave the apartment. But apart from that, he tried to convince himself that he had behaved as any worthy neighbor would behave if he had heard that scratching, if he had been summoned, even, to go to the dead man's apartment, or if, for whatever reason, it had maybe only seemed like that to him. Even if that were the case, yes. Since it must be right for a person to make sure, and not be indifferent to harm which, of course, the owner himself—that is to say, the dead man—probably wouldn't feel, but which, even so, simply cannot be ignored.

Then he had the urge to see and smell again that little piece of notepaper with *her* handwriting on it—to touch it, caress it . . . it would be at least a little easier for him if he could feel *her* in the marks on the page and believe that it was really *she* who had written that line. He could no longer remember her face. It had somehow dissolved in a fog. He knew only that she had black hair, that her little mouth made a sweet little pout, that maybe this was why her face seemed a bit pale, and that she was naked from the waist down. He also remembered the black opal necklace—and to think that he had gone to get the neighbors like some cowardly fool while she, the way she was . . . was waiting for him in Kremavc's apartment—it stung him afresh each time. So with a sigh he stood up and searched through the pockets of his jacket. But the letter wasn't there. Nor was it in his pants pockets, nor in his bathrobe. And yet here and there, in this pocket and that one, he thought he smelled, clear and fresh, the scent of Shalimar. But even so, the letter was not there anymore. It was nowhere. Not on the floor of the wardrobe. Not anywhere in the bed and not next to it. He tried to calm down and think about what could have happened. Even the possibility that it had maybe fallen out of his pocket and his wife had found it and said nothing . . . or maybe, being so thin and light, it had somehow gotten lost somewhere beneath the wardrobe or the nightstand or the chest of drawers, and he tried in vain despite all these scattered thoughts to convince himself that it would turn up sooner or later. He would tell his wife that there were some strange characters out on the streets who force their nonsense on you and you forget if at some time or other you happen to stick one of these items in your pocket. But his wife was not the issue. He didn't really care what she would think. So he went back into the living room and searched there, not bothering to conceal that he was looking for something. And said nothing when she asked what had gotten into him . . . and kept on poking around and going through things even when he had run out of places to look. He was distraught; he couldn't believe it, couldn't accept it; he was overcome with sadness, with an almost painful dejection, confusion and dread of all that is elusive and incomprehensible in events, things, people—in apartments too, and in the streets and the avenues, in the hum and the rumble, the silence and the smoke—and in that which follows. Dr. Pavlovski would in all likelihood deem it foolish to run from yourself and the truth. But now there was no time for Dr. Pavlovski to speak, because Valent had to search for the letter—and for Shulamite. He could feel that his wife's eyes were following him, that she found him strange, that he was getting on her nerves, and even that he was making her a little worried. At one point she said he'd become impossible to live with, but she didn't persist with it, didn't go any further, as if she had simply run out of words and now could only be silently amazed. And not understand. And he would have to use all his strength if he wanted to explain anything to her, for reaching her was like coming out of a hazy heaviness, a groggy daze, from which it was necessary to first regain consciousness and then struggle for words which could never serve their purpose no matter how they were strung together. There was too much lying on top of them. Too much of everything had piled up over the years . . . so that now, deeply submerged, as in a putrid ooze, and warped from one thing or another, they were virtually unusable. If, for example, he had begun: Look, I am searching for the thing that is missing between us, missing everywhere, she would certainly hear something different; and were he to go on and say that this thing is called Shulamite, she would believe it was aimed against her, against her age, and other such things not worth going into.

The morning dragged on and on; he could hardly remember such a morning. At some point it was his wife who finally went down to get the newspaper. And when she came back she did not mention anyone stopping her or speaking to her. True, he didn't ask. But she probably would have said something on her own, as she always had before, since familiarity of any sort between even the closest neighbors in the building was hardly the order of the day.

But she didn't even open the newspaper. It just lay there on the table . . . It lay there obtruding on his range of vision so that he had trouble looking away from it in a seemingly casual manner; it was difficult to keep casting his eyes in some other direction so they wouldn't land on the big, bold front-page headlines, while at the same time making sure that his wife did not notice this turning and averting of his eyes. He must not look. Must not read anything. Not even a word. Just to glance at the accompanying pictures might spell disaster. Since it might say that there was no hope left for some little girl; or maybe that new findings on the Brežine murder investigation point to a still-unidentified man who often takes evening strolls in the neighborhood . . . All sorts of notions swarmed through his head. Confusing him. And wouldn't go away. So he just got up. Without saying a word, he just left the apartment and, afraid of meeting the Marzis, fairly ran to the elevator as if pressed for time, even with his injured foot.

It was empty. The doors had barely closed when it started moving. Up. He thought how strange it was that the doors had so quickly closed behind him and that he had wanted to go down. This was not the first time, of course, that he was forced to go up to some higher floor before going down to the ground floor. This had gotten on his nerves more than once, but it didn't suit the image of a business executive to make a fuss about such things. So on this occasion, too, when the elevator finally stopped and the doors opened and nobody was there and nobody got on, he nevertheless waited obligingly and patiently, and only after some time had passed did he press the button for the ground floor once again.

But the elevator did not move.

The doors remained open.

He kept on pressing the button, but to no avail.

From what he could see from inside the elevator, it had gone up to the top floor, the loft directly beneath the roof of the building. The large, unpartitioned space, segmented by rows of stocky four-sided pillars, appeared extremely unwelcoming. Lonely. A sort of gloomy tiredness seemed to dominate. A little light came in from the outside through the murky glass of a narrow slit of window that probably ran uninterrupted along each wall. His attention was drawn to the black, silver-lined drawings on the pillars . . . He was actually surprised by how much room was up there; judging from the pornographic drawings, this must be a meeting place, at least sporadically, for who knows what sort of urban rabble. Besides the reclining, spread-eagle nudes, the interlocked and variously coupled pairs, he could make out a number of unfamiliar names, as well as the words SATANAS and EEEEVILL . . . This was, it was true, the kind of thing you saw everywhere around the city, scrawled in underpasses, on buildings and walls, but here the effect was different, very different. There were no light fixtures or electric fittings visible on the uniformly unfinished, unplastered concrete walls. Floating dust was visible in the angled sheaf of light that fell from the window into the shadows between the pillars.

The elevator could not be made to move.

Although the ceiling light in the elevator was still on.

Also the lights in the buttons, which he now pressed one after another and at random, would light up each time and then go out. But nothing else was working.

There was nobody visible among the pillars. He tried to console himself with the thought that maybe someone had simply made a mistake and pressed the wrong button . . . maybe there was some silly prank involved, too. After which everything just broke down . . . He pressed the alarm button and one or two others, all the while infuriated by the idea that now he would have to limp and wheeze his way down who knows how many stairs, and he really was going to let Oletič have it, for all this and everything else. Other people, too, who might be waiting for this damn elevator below, would also be sure to complain to the building manager, or so he hoped, as he tried to shake off the quite silly uneasiness that had taken hold of him—because of those obscene drawings and inscriptions, he told himself, this quite ordinary nonsense—and he peered out into the loft . . . The person who pushed the button might now be waiting, might even be watching him . . . with nobody else around. Certainly, the loft seemed rather lonely and gloomy, and at the same time, clearly anyone, whether from the building or from the outside, could get to it easily enough. He could no longer believe in some coincidental mistake or malfunction. Still, he took comfort in the fact that in a building such as this, even if not fully occupied, a malfunctioning elevator couldn't go unnoticed for long and that somebody, maybe Oletič, would probably very soon be coming up to see what was wrong.

But time just dragged on.

The air was stuffy and dusty beneath the low, overheated ceiling. And thoughts about the staircase, which might be very close by, were becoming, despite the graffiti and his anxiousness, ever more frequent.

Still, for a brief moment he thought he saw someone slink into a nearby corner.

But it was impossible to see further between the pillars beyond the walls of the elevator shaft.

He took a step or two out of the elevator, but did not notice or hear anything. Heat pulsated from the low concrete ceiling, which was no higher than the ceiling in the elevator.

Then he limped, determinedly, all around the elevator shaft.

But there was no staircase.

He made a bigger circle through the loft, with no less determination, but there was still no staircase.

The elevator still just sat there gaping—it could be seen now and then between the pillars, which stood in a pattern of interwoven rows . . . and on one of the pillars, written in large, runny, brownish-red letters, was the word SHULAMITH . . . Flabbergasted, horrified, he stood a while staring at this inscription and something about menstrual blood went whirling through his mind. Although the effect was childish. But also terrifying. And exalting, all at once . . . there was a secret society, then, maybe people from the building, maybe from the neighborhood, a sect—his mind was racing—who knows what sort of lunatics, murderers . . . Somewhere nearby, right next to him, behind his back, he sensed what seemed like a presence . . . and with a prickling in his skin, in his scalp, a dark jolt through his thoughts, he turned around . . . but nobody was there. Not in the light, or by the pillar, or in the shadows . . . There was only tiny shimmering dust floating everywhere, all around.

In some places between the pillars lay a deep gloom. Almost darkness. A bitter taste, unpleasantly dusty, was forming in his dehydrated mouth. He was finding it hard to breathe. He could feel sweat beading from every pore. And each time he moved or took a step, there was a stirring somewhere out there in the silence. Also near the pillar. Also in the shadows. It pressed in his ears, against his anxious heart . . . and the vertiginous dust twirled and swayed, and the loft seemed at moments vast and endless and somehow always the same whether you looked in this or that or any direction, with the lines of pillars merging one into the other and then branching off again at irregular intervals, maybe diagonally, maybe curving away, each going its own way. The elevator was no more to be seen. Here and there, always the same, the narrow slit of window glowered down at him.

13

He tried to ease himself into the guise of an observer who just happens to be walking around, just happens to be looking at one thing or another, and if something catches his attention, well, it might be interesting or then again it might not be. In spite of his limp, he tried to regulate his steps at a suitably leisurely pace, and placed his hands behind his back to enhance the image of calmly confident loft-strolling nonchalance. Nothing could be seen through the narrow window opening, which in fact turned out to be a built-in glass wall that ran along the top of the surrounding walls. Shimmering dust danced in front of it. In places, too, it was as if it had just been set whirling by a barely perceptible gust of air, or something similarly inaudible and invisible, which could then twist and glide between the pillars, along the walls, and, here and there, through the beams of light. And occasionally a feeling stirred in his head that it was all in a way unpredictable, that it was hiding much more than could be seen or heard, that the thing must be sprawling in the background with a sort of mute shapelessness, and that people were under its control. Clearly, the drawings, sometimes with the genitals emphasized in red, and the different captions, in all their numerous variations, signified one and the same madness, one and the same belief . . . The silver-lined black of the letters, regardless of whether the words were copied out, neatly drawn, or merely scrawled, exposed without mercy the barrenness or mere pretense of meanings for everyday use. Claudius, Cilla, Betty, Marina, Tadeusz . . . even the word LOVE could, in such gruesome writing, mean the very opposite; even the words GOD and ALLELUIA seemed perverted and ominous. No matter what was written—it could be ordinary, big, little, passionate, succulent, but mainly it was names, names—everything took on a different meaning.

The only inscription he did not notice anywhere else was SHULAMITH. The simple fact that it had been written near the elevator and in a color other than black made him curious. He was sorry, in fact, that he had not inspected those blood-like runny letters and the picture that accompanied them closely enough. They might have concealed some message, some hint; certainly, this was not some chance anomaly and he probably shouldn't have overlooked it . . . it gave him no peace. It kept returning to his thoughts, entangling itself in the meaning of everything else he looked at, everything he read on the pillars and walls around him, and something about menstrual blood, about a *campfire dance,* and everything got twisted together into a craving to touch those erect little nipples. And the farther away he went from it, the more powerfully it pulled him back, to SHULAMITH . . . but he did not know exactly which way was backward or forward, or which direction he in fact had to turn, since his view was obstructed by long, narrow squares or trapezoids formed by the pillars, while the spaces between them kept splitting and diverging, so he had to limp along in circles, and the building evidently divided at very irregular angles into different wings that up here formed an unpartitioned whole; and therefore with all these pillars and with the sidewalls running now in this direction, now in that direction, it was all a confusion, since his mouth was getting horribly drier and stickier from the dust and the heat; and he wanted to believe something was guiding him, to believe, that is, in some foolishness, since the room was somehow getting turned around, since every so often without him noticing *forward* became *backward,* or vice versa; or it seemed the same in all directions as he looked around and turned around, trying at the same time to ease his anxiety when something dark slipped in front of this or that drawing or only seemed to, when there was a clack like a footstep and the beams of light flickered between pillars and shadows as dark corners yawned in the distance; when at the same time in his overheated brain loomed something about a deep, delicate *surgical incision* in a slight curve from the chin to below the left ear, sparking that dance, merciless and inescapable, that dimming into confusion, even short, desperate attempts to resist, to fight back, to disentangle himself . . . "Enough!" he said out loud, though to no one but himself. "Get lost!" he ordered. And listened. And thought how ashamed he would be if anybody had heard him. "Go away!" he growled at a pillar nonetheless, as if in ridicule of himself. And for some reason, he picked up a little black can and paintbrush off the floor in front of him. At that very moment, from the corner of his eye, he noticed something . . . In the light. By the window. It looked like a little girl . . . a cold shiver ran through him. "Come here, come here . . ." he stammered into the air. Then nothing could be seen anymore.

Even so, he started retreating, walking backwards; he didn't dare turn his back on the light. Although this didn't give him any assurance, any certainty—his view was partly obstructed by one corner, and then another, and then by an increasingly jagged line of pillars and drawings. All his thoughts had evaporated. Only the fleeting, sketchy image of a little girl kept appearing on the horizon . . . as it got hazier and shakier from pillar to pillar, he had to support himself, to creep along, first with one shoulder then the other, making sure the black paint didn't spill from the little can, and look all around yet somehow not make any noise.

Then he caught sight of someone over to his left.

For certain this time.

In a dark corner. Not far away.

Sure enough, the very next moment he saw that it was the building manager, Oletič . . . who was chewing something but trying to hide it. His cheeks taut, his lips pursed in a tight pout under a horseshoe mustache, he looked out. And said nothing. With much relief, Valent realized that Oletič must have called the elevator from up in the loft and maybe was going to take it down when for some unknown reason he took cover.

"The elevator . . ." he said, his mouth dry, trying with difficulty to project something like calm fortitude over there to Oletič. "It's jammed, I think . . . So I guess the loft is where people put stuff that can't be used anymore—the names, I mean, and all this . . ." He nodded in the direction of the inscriptions and drawings on the pillars; he wanted to make a kind of joke . . . and he didn't know what to with this idiotic can, a child's paint can. "Is there a child with you?" He tried to compose his nerves; he even held the can up a bit as if it were the main reason he was asking the question. Oletič neither nodded yes nor shook his head no, but for a brief moment there was something black hanging out of his pout—it looked like a drool-covered mouse tail . . . but whatever it was, as if embarrassed, he hurriedly sucked it back in, drool and all. Apparently, it was too big to just gulp down, so he gazed out poutily and rolled that something-or-other around in his mouth and evidently didn't know what else to do. Valent, of course, would have liked to know for sure what it was, but he couldn't just keep staring at a person's mouth, so he lowered the paint can and looked around, partly in embarrassment over his possibly unfortunate joke, but also partly looking for what had seemed, perhaps only to him, to be an outline or drawing of *her* . . . and just then he heard the soft, plump sound of Oletič spitting something out, and an instant later, a splat on the floor. But when he looked at the floor around Oletič, he could see nothing that looked as if it had been spat out. Maybe Oletič had stepped on it. Or kicked it away. He was still staring, fairly glowering, and eventually muttered out, "What child?" As if from guilt, the feigned resentment was audible. "And what if it's you who's bringing them here, Kosmina?" he added, and forced his expression into a look of steely suspicion. "And all of this . . ." He glanced at the paint can and, gesturing toward the pillars, attempted to give him a look of accusatory contempt. Oletič's familiarity, his dropping the Mr., was in itself enough to pain Valent. And then, like the lord of the manor inspecting damage to his property, he started circling the pillars and shaking his head and generally acting as if he had just nabbed one of the hooligans who had been, as it were, befouling the place. To Valent, the can in his hand was a disagreeable nuisance, to be sure, but he couldn't just set it down now. So he followed Oletič toward the light and said, in an entirely justified reproach, "Now listen here . . ." But Oletič, without turning around, as if speaking to himself and not seeing any need to interrupt his assessment of the damage, simply muttered at the pillar in front of him, "So I have to listen to you now too, is that it . . . ?" Which struck Valent as ridiculously conceited and insolent—but the can and paintbrush were certainly not helping, so the best thing would be to convince him right away that he had simply gotten the wrong idea. A person can just happen to pick something like that up off the floor. And doesn't know himself why he picked it up. Something like that could easily happen, of course, even to *him*, to Oletič. But it wouldn't be fair to him either if people just started casting aspersions right away and condemning him because of them. But Oletič was being far too pompous now for Valent to be able to say anything like that. Then too, he was dressed (in the shadowy corner Valent hadn't noticed before) in something like a uniform. Which was clearly much too big for him: the pants were gathered around the ankles and got in the way when he walked. The vest was not only too narrow for his broad shoulders; it was also, clearly, too long. The color of the uniform reminded Valent of heavy, wet earth . . . and it dawned on him, unpleasantly, that he had more than once seen people around the city who were dressed something like that. Who were most likely cemetery workers. He even remembered thinking at funerals that as soon as those people with their gloomy earth-colored uniforms and their gloomy earth-colored faces surround your bed or coffin, it's not a joke anymore, there's no more hope, and you can't expect them to give you any help or pity. He felt the urge to say, straight out, in a forceful enough, deep enough, masculine voice: We're old, Mr. Oletič, we're old—or something similar, but this idea, too, even before he opened his mouth, he abandoned. And as if he had simply had enough, he put down the paint can . . . which Oletič noticed immediately. And looking meaningfully grim, went without a word to get it. Valent of course would have just left him there, paint can and all, had he known where to find the stairs. That would have given him immense satisfaction. But as it was, he was forced—although he pretended it was by chance and he was just looking at the drawings and inscriptions—to stand there a while, wait for him, and then follow him at a distance of two or three paces. The building manager, meanwhile, paint can in hand, clearly felt himself now more important even; he examined the graffiti-covered pillars with even greater thoroughness, wagging his head, every now and then, as if too revolted for words, clucking his tongue in displeasure. Thus they proceeded from pillar to pillar. Valent, increasingly racked with fatigue, couldn't rid himself of the feeling that Oletič was merely feigning all this and in fact had something to hide.

"Is it really the first time you've seen this?" He at last broke the silence, fed up with it all. But Oletič merely glanced at him, as if he was hardly worth his attention, and then went over to the next pillar. After which more time passed. After which Valent again had to swallow his rage and an impatience that was already somewhat mitigated, most likely from fatigue, as well as hope for any possible relief at the first suitable opportunity. They had circled another two or three, or maybe even five or more, pillars in this manner when at last he saw the elevator.

Still immobile, it gaped wide open into the twilight of the loft.

Still the light in the ceiling burned, immobile.

But all the same, Valent hurried over to it, though at the same time he thought how foolish it was to hurry like that; and then he again pressed one button after another, and was soon pressing them randomly, although he knew it was foolish and Oletič was watching him.

"What's wrong with it?" he muttered, furious, even hitting the button panel. And then in a much louder, but still rather controlled voice, speaking slowly for emphasis, he reminded Oletič that the elevator should probably be put back into operation and that the people who were now waiting in vain for it below would certainly have something to say. But it did no good. Oletič calmly circled the pillar he had just inspected, then moved to the next one and was, it appeared, making some comparison, and only after he had finished this long and most likely needless comparison did he proceed with slow and pensive, confident steps, not ceasing to examine things along the way to the elevator. When he entered, he pulled a little device out of his pocket, a kind of remote control, perhaps. There was a bit of black paint from the paint can on his fat stubby fingers, and a few red spots were visible, too.

"There are people waiting below," Valent repeated, in a more conciliatory tone, and as if to explain his earlier impatience, and with his eyes focused somewhere on Oletič's forehead, he tried to give himself a little dignity.

"Just where do you think you are?" Oletič snarled dismissively, and evidently with the help of the little device in his paint-stained hand (and maybe not all the stains were fresh ones), he turned the elevator back on. He might have done so much earlier of course, but Valent now had no will to make the point and maybe argue with this man or whatever else might follow. He had never liked Oletič one bit—he hated his yellowish-reddish, always even, cropped hair, his droopy horseshoe mustache and short stubbly beard, and those thick, bullishly humped shoulders, not to mention the man's swaggering self-importance . . . his gray, fat eyes had this unpleasant way of always rotating and shifting back and forth and then every so often freezing as if to challenge or threaten you, impertinently piercing straight into your eyes and then the very next moment, as if confused again and unsure, pulling away. His round, flushed face was unfailingly cross and disdainful and at the same time furtively watchful . . .

But the elevator was moving now.

They both pressed a button and Valent was able to remove himself a little from the Oletič's disagreeable nearness by assuming what was indeed his usual guise for elevators, a nonchalance that included not looking at anyone, watching the numbers above the doors, checking his watch, and waiting, with just a touch of impatience, for the impending exit.

He exited in silence, without saying goodbye.

Only as he was limping down the empty hallway toward his apartment did it occur to him that nobody had stopped the elevator, at least not above the fifteenth floor—they must have gotten fed up with waiting, which was undoubtedly Oletič's fault, and he would tell him too, at the next available opportunity; he would make a point of it, and in the same breath mention Oletič's salary, which as building manager he naturally takes every month out of their rents.

The Marzis, fortunately, were not in the hallway.

14

From somewhere his wife brought the news that "Mr." Mario had gotten rich. Overnight. Nobody knew how. Just like that, he became wealthy and moved away—where, she didn't know. Some island, she supposed, and seemed convinced of it, or one of those fashionable mountain resorts where they do everything for you—this she also deemed acceptable—or at least some prestigious neighborhood with, of course, a villa with a garden and lots of greenery and trees all around.

He was just about to doze off when she came back from who knows where, her face pale and eyes sparkling, and started telling him all about it.

Naturally, the story astounded him, disturbed him, and naturally, he thought immediately, as if to console himself, that it was all just gossip and the whole thing was most likely fabricated.

But just the thought of the possibility, as small and improbable as it seemed, cast a pall over his face, so he preferred to say nothing and only try to listen and nod now and then with something like a smile—which could also mean incredulity, or indulgent forbearance toward all that had managed to get mixed into his wife's story from who knows which of her soap-opera fantasies. Still, she did seem quite sure about what she was saying. To no avail he tried to convince himself that in fact this was (it was more than obvious) some rehashed old story, the sort that people dish out big and small every day at every step; for the simple thought that this "Mr." Mario might really perhaps . . . that there was some truth to the story . . . it got his stomach all tangled up in knots, as if wormy maggots were twisting around down there inside him. Then his wife really did start to fantasize about how "Mr." Mario had maybe always been wealthy, and how he had—like many eccentrics of that sort, for a short time and for his own amusement—assumed the role of a humble pensioner-meal deliveryman; she'd swear under oath that she had always sensed in him that profound high-class nobility, that superior quality, which no matter how carefully hidden always shines through, and which she can sense immediately, no doubt about it, since surely she knows how to tell pearls from pebbles or what have you . . .

Then she started tidying up; she was actually just shifting things around needlessly. "It all comes true for some people," she sighed. "Some people can do it; some people find their way . . ." She had to know how bitterly this was grating on him. He might have told her that mere wealth meant nothing in and of itself, that it was all insanity, a kind of mass delusion, but instead he went silently into the bedroom as if oblivious to all her empty fantasizing. If the key had been in the door, he might even have locked it behind him. So things happen to other people, so they happen somewhere else . . . the world has always gone mad over such stories—he could have told her all this and thrown in something about pornography too, about the god of the streets, about the frescoes at the Little Paradise . . . but she would have understood it all, would have seen it all, differently. There was no help for it. Even the thought of Brežine sickened him. Mammon . . . and the ancient, centuries-old darkness within and among humankind.

He tried to fall asleep, but his wife kept poking around outside, moving things back and forth, and every so often he thought the bedroom door was somehow opening by itself, but each time he glanced over there in alarm, the door was still closed . . . and he kept mulling things over again and again and turning and doubting and this Mario business seemed, as if on its own, to tie in with the Kremavc apartment, with Oletič; and he kept asking himself why such a "gentleman" as "Mr." Mario would call him in the middle of the night, and where did this letter come from, and who in fact sent it, and for what purpose—certainly, he sensed there was something contemptible, something sordid here—he did not for a moment believe that this "Mr." Mario could be any kind of a true gentleman and so he could only be some thrill-seeker dressed as a pornography dealer and an entirely disreputable employee of the pensioners' meal service. His wife was undoubtedly confused by that. Also, the SHULAMITH inscription in the loft and all those names, as well as Oletič's stained hands and his idiotic charade, might all belong here . . . He didn't know how. He didn't know why. And the girl . . . He listened to his wife in the other room, and to the wall of the Kremavc apartment; distractingly, the hum of the city pressed at the windows; doubts about the reality of this sudden affluence entwined with an oppressive feeling of tangledness, of powerlessness, and an apprehension that gnawed at him and could no longer be simply dismissed. Then for a while he must have been dreaming—there was a fresco from the Little Paradise . . . and somewhere there, to the delight and amusement of everyone assembled, a naked girl, drenched in what was probably honey, was dancing some debauched dance; one of them was gold and plump and smiled a plump golden smile; a green lady giggled loudly, obviously trying to draw attention to herself; someone was a bull with bloodshot eyes, or something similar, with long strands of drool dripping from his mouth; one or another of these chosen mortals was feigning a tame casualness, while someone else was dozing soundly through the whole thing and the twins with little goat tails were running and skipping silently back and forth on tiptoe probably chasing a fly or something, which was an undoubtedly huge, undoubtedly terribly disturbing unpleasantness, though to all appearances nobody else was paying it any mind. "Look! A fly or something . . ." Valent blurted out, and at once realized he had committed a terrible faux pas . . . that he had thus aroused the others' contempt, which of course they did not show, because in a temple and during a ritual one does not show such a thing. He knew for a certainty that he must leave now, that although the others were silent and seemingly oblivious, they cruelly demanded it, and that he must by no means simply stand there and wait, consoling himself with the thought that he had pointed to the truth with all good intentions and that at least someone among the assembled would be at least a little pleased. But it didn't look like it. They were waiting in silence, with averted eyes, for him to get out of there, no matter how, no matter with what kind of a face, since a word is not a fly, since a temple is not a stable . . . He was already trying, too, to put everything right by his piously devoted concentration on the girl's dance—and in this humble concentration he found the beginning of a hope that perhaps she herself, most wondrously honeyed and adorable, would, mainly because of the words he had spoken, because of all the wordless dissemblance among those present, dance right over to him, would come get him, and offer him her little hand dripping with honey, and raise him in her favor and in her love . . . It lay like a weight inside his chest. His wife made no sound. And right at this moment the bedroom door was again opening—or closing—as if of its own accord . . . What remained, then, was that no one had licked any honey and he had not left, although of course he was no longer there either and none of it was here . . . Evening was falling. And in the swollen din of the city it was impossible to detect any human voice or, indeed, any living sound.

He started when his wife entered the room, although she came in slowly, almost stealthily. From the way she walked he could tell she was sedated.

"There's somebody here," she whispered, as if concentrating on something. "In the living room . . ."

He lifted himself on his elbows. And looked at her. And couldn't be sure if he had really managed to hide his fear.

"The TV's dead," she added as an explanation. And then just said nothing, waiting.

He tried to make himself stay calm. To believe it was just the pills making her like that. Washed down with a little cognac. So he took his time getting up, sitting in the bed for a bit as if to indulge himself, and pretended that he entirely understood about the television, and only then, as if he was coolly indifferent more than anything, did he stand up.

"Come, Olga," he tried to give her a smile. She moved her hand away; she would not let him hold it. She even took a step back. "Why don't we go in and turn on the TV?" he explained to her.

"Oh, no!" she shook her head back and forth as if afraid. "We mustn't . . ."

"Why won't you give me your hand, Olga?" he asked in a casual way, with a shrug, as if he were just asking—he was trying by all means to stay calm.

"Did you see someone? Is that it?"

Again she shook her head.

Then, as if confused and in a fury and determined all at once, he went into the living room without her.

He did not see anyone there . . .

The only thing that caught his eye was the ebony statuette of the naked girl, which was on the little table between the stuffed armchairs. Usually it stood in the glass cabinet. His wife must have moved it while cleaning.

For a moment, he felt relieved. Sometimes, he thought, a person just imagines he sees something . . .

Nor was there anything wrong with the television. He turned it on, tried different channels, tested the sound and the color, then readjusted everything back to the normal volume and tone and switched to his wife's favorite channel. The show, of course, was one of her soap operas, about an old villa and the people who lived there . . .

Just to be sure, he looked around.

His wife was still in the bedroom.

He even called to her.

No response.

The soap-opera sounds supposedly signified restful comfort, and maybe, too, a certainty about death and the hereafter—but he decided to turn off the television, to listen instead to the silence stretching over the hum outside and to try and believe that what you don't see or hear maybe doesn't exist . . . although from the ceiling and walls and cabinets and objects came silence, like the distance hidden behind the planes of appearances, the same silence even came from the black conceitedness of the girl. He tried to think that his wife had merely been imagining things, but it was no use . . . and there must be water leaking from the faucet in the bathroom, although a little earlier, right after he turned off the television, he was almost certain he had heard no dripping. He told himself that he simply hadn't been paying attention, that his wife must have forgotten to shut off the faucet, so he got up and, a step or two from the bathroom door, he stopped and listened, holding his breath, and saw that the door was slightly ajar and it was dark inside. He could hear the faucet making its usual hissing sound from the water pressure. Meanwhile, thoughts about the scalpel, and about "Mr." Mario suddenly getting rich, flashed through his mind, but even so he moved forward, with heavy, slow steps, determinedly pushed open the door, and stood there just for a moment and looked around, deliberately not turning the light on. There was quite enough light coming from the living room. He turned off the faucet without the least anxiety.

On his way back he looked in the front hall, reconnected the telephone, at the same time checking to see that the front door was locked.

This time he definitely wanted to prove something to himself and to his wife . . . although the simple fact that he had the courage—the courage, that is, to walk around the apartment like that, or just sit there into the evening, when the walls and the ceiling and the cabinets and all of it was silent, though maybe only on the outside, for show, cozy and homey.

It angered him that, having alarmed him, she didn't come out of the bedroom, and when, after some time, he looked in on her, he found that she had simply lain down on the bed in her pink bathrobe. She was just lying there on her stomach and was most likely playing deaf when he, sure that she wasn't asleep yet, spoke to her. It was horrible to see her like that, sprawled out, with her bathrobe gathered up over her big rear end and wedged between fat-rippled thighs. She looked like a kind of decoy, as if everything that—over the years, despite all changes inside and out, as if for all time—had signified her, had somehow passed, or vanished, or died away . . . He decided to just leave her as she was. And went back to his armchair. And soon noticed that the curtain by the window was moving seemingly on its own. True, it stirred only every so often . . . The window was shut. So were all the doors. The kitchen entrance, too, had a curtain, but the curtain there did not move. So his thoughts turned to air circulation, vents, and the like . . . and from the corner of his eye he perceived a flickering in the kitchen, as from the quivering light of a little flame.

Now he did not hesitate.

He dashed into the kitchen. And found a nearly extinguished, melted candle on the table. Without a second thought, he put it out—and that moment felt as if a shadow had fallen. Chill. Dark. Somehow stifling. There was nobody, nothing, in any of the corners—despite the tingling he felt, as if he had a fleeting, uncertain sense of a presence, or perhaps it was merely apprehension or fear, since he didn't know what it was or why it was there or anything particular at all, since he mostly just wanted to run away; since it seemed to him that his wife, too, was in fact a corpse, and that the walls and kitchen table and everything around was lying in wait, dark and deathly silent. He took a breath and held it; he stood up straight and as slowly as he could left the kitchen and tried to ease the beating of his heart, tried to ease his crisscrossed, bewildered mind; then he sat down as if it were nothing, though he was still shaking and tense, and the curtain was moving again, and the statuette of the girl was almost certainly looking in at least a slightly different direction.

He also tried to blame his wife for the lit candle, but it didn't work . . . his thoughts were almost turning into images, into voices; things were exposed in them, as dreams are exposed. He made an effort to look at the statuette and consider its contours and the girl-ish beauty captured in them and through them—only this, only thus—and to forget the other thing, dismiss the feeling that something would still reveal itself—maybe it would come from behind him, from behind the curtain, from the walls around him, or all of a sudden, from the evening; maybe without contour or color, without image, without voice or scent—in other words, all of sudden, when he couldn't do anything but gaze at the ebony that had been carved, polished, caressed into the image of a girl and think of the adorably rounded contours of girls and forget about the one before his eyes. The one that might confuse him . . . make him look around, make him listen intently . . . That would make him tense, his thoughts would take on strange shapes, with voices and whispers and strange meanings, something owlish. Yet he tried to focus his eyes and ears on the statuette, which the artist has given an adorably curvy girlish torso, an innocently parted bottom over her folded legs, the barely budding but already-awakened breasts; the hands are posed on her skirt in a beautifully gentle way, and the hair, smooth as silk, is delicately rendered, and the face has just the right trace of coquettish sorrow; the eyes, though, are dull and dead and wooden, but everything else is nearly perfect, enough, that is, to fill the evening, enough to invite his thoughts and drive away these horrible feelings of running, rummaging, twisting, grimacing, or wide-eyed staring, and the doubts and suspicions and the sudden bang on Kremavc's wall . . .

Which was followed by another. Two or three seconds later . . .

And a third one. As if someone had started hammering nails, slowly, or lazily, or each time reconsidering before striking, and then there was a rasping sound, the same way, slow, as if the person making it was tired, then also the clattering of a chair . . . it was unusually annoying, unusually hard on the nerves, which jumped as if overstrained at every individual bang and clatter. Even worse was hearing the sawing, which stopped, it seemed, after varying intervals—that got him out of the armchair, but in the front hall he changed his mind and went back and sat down, but then went over to the window and back again; meanwhile, what sounded like a log of firewood fell on the floor over there with a resounding crash, after which the saw started up again and then stopped, then from the same saw came exactly nine short weak rasps, and then a long one that died away as if it had dozed off, then started up again with those nine short rasps—he'd like to rush over there himself, like to do some sawing, even hammer a nail the way it should be hammered, and move a cabinet or whatever it was they were pushing and pulling in starts and stops somewhere farther away in the apartment, into the background, so that it dug into the floor with a screech . . . This time, obviously, no one was trying to hide anything. It could all mean that somebody had just moved in, or that people were (at an inappropriate hour, it's true) straightening up or reorganizing things after Kremavc's death, were it not, of course, for that oppressively sluggish slowness, that weariness, sticky and heavy, which seemed to have some hazily displaced, indistinct, rambling meaning, and even after things got quiet, became still and didn't start up again, and it gave him a stiffening chill in every nerve.

Quite unexpectedly, as if in mid-swing of the hammer, a sepulchral silence had fallen.

Now not even the slightest sound could be heard.

As if whoever it was had frozen in absolute motionlessness. Only the muffled, distant hum of the city droned on outside the window, evenly and unbrokenly, over his tense waiting.

And suddenly there was the click of a latch.

A moment later, someone was knocking at his door. A man called softly: "Neighbor? Oh, neighbor?" There was no trace of agitation in the voice. Mainly, it sounded courteous.

Maybe it was Marzi.

What if he had been disturbed by the noise from the Kremavc apartment and now wanted Valent to go with him to see what was going on? He might have seen the light on through the peephole . . .

and now, clearly, had no intention of giving up, although Valent neither answered nor stirred from the armchair. The only thing he thought was that the incautious, imprudent Marzi had perhaps tried to open Kremavc's door himself, and of course that was when the people inside froze and went quiet, as if they'd been brought to a halt, and that for some reason this time he really didn't feel like getting involved in other people's affairs.

But the person at the door was persistent. He even began to plead, to pester him, saying, for example, "Neighbor, I know you're still up," and then, "Well, okay, fine," because maybe he, too, wouldn't want to open his door someday–but he believed people should be willing to help each other, encourage each other. It was in fact peculiar that he would keep persisting like that, keep talking like that, as was the fact that he could be heard and understood with perfect clarity, though there was no doubt that he was speaking in a very soft voice. And this pleading, this quiet, even at times whispered, persuasion only made Valent more resistant—but his whole head went abuzz when the man at the door started pressing the doorbell (short and more or less courteous rings, to be sure) and simply did not want to stop pressing it.

"There's somebody at the . . ." his wife drew out the words between yawns; obviously, this ringing had gotten her out of bed. And she left the bedroom and went right to the foyer, and before he could remind her that it was not very wise to open the door to people at night, she had already opened it and was assuring the person in her tongue-tied way that it wasn't so very late, that really it was no inconvenience, that Vali and she were accustomed to . . . as the man at the door offered his apologies and explained that he was a neighbor, a *friend* of Vali's, and he couldn't help but . . .

"Oh, you're a . . . ?"

"Pavlovski," he interjected.

Valent went cold . . . at that name, his heart skipped a beat; he felt weak and couldn't breathe as his wife drawled on in a sugary tone about what a wonderful surprise it was, "truly, Doctor, you know . . . Vaaalii!" she called, almost like a yawn, and then he saw the two of them as if through a haze, both smiling at him, coming toward him . . . a fat man dressed in a sort of earth-brown uniform with a bow tie that was tied too tightly . . . but almost as if inebriated, he offered his hand for a handshake, and gave the man a nod, letting himself be patted jovially on the shoulder, while he heard his wife falling over herself to offer the man a seat, and a cognac, and the explanation that sometimes Vali, you know, just dozes off in his chair . . . After which the man—maybe the same fat man with the toupee he had seen in Brežine—sprawled out in the armchair opposite, one leg crossed over the other, and calmly peered into Valent's eyes with a riveting gaze. In the meantime, Valent, for no apparent reason, was moving the statuette of the ebony girl.

"So how are things? I mean, how are you feeling?" he asked straight out, his eyes deep and big, as if he had every right to make such personal inquiries. One could hear something cynical, perhaps disinterested, in that thick voice of his, which acted as an additional force along with those eyes, so that Valent found it impossible to refuse or dispel any question he posed. All he could do, yet not too easily, was look away, look for his pipe, and grab it as if it were a life preserver. His wife, meanwhile, all wobbly and simpering, had served the cognac and now babbled almost unintelligibly about how nice it was for the Doctor to have taken the time . . . and that she'd put the coffee on too, if no one had any objection.

The "Doctor" clearly had no objection.

"I hear you're quite the cook." He was certainly making himself at home.

She only giggled, as if she really was stupid.

"Your husband is always singing your praises," he continued as she went toward the kitchen. "'Pavlovski,' he says, 'my wife's a virtuoso in the kitchen!'"

Valent had to struggle to light his pipe. His hands were heavy, as if cast in lead, and didn't want to obey him.

"Well, now I've been told to look in on you, to see what's wrong," the brazen fellow said, with an easygoing yet condescending click of his tongue, and with the obvious intention that Valent's wife be able to follow the conversation, as he now assumed a more subdued and, as it were, directly confidential tone. Valent looked anxiously at the fleshy face in front of him, at those fleshy shovel-like hands, and feverishly, frantically, tried to find the best possible solution . . .

In the meantime his wife minced in with the coffee.

"Madam, forgive me!" Their "neighbor" shot up, as if he had been waiting for just the moment when the coffee was brought in. "If I may be so . . ."—he quickly, and maybe only for show, ran his hands over his pockets—". . . bold as to offer you this trifle . . ." He was breathing heavily.

And from his pocket he pulled out a box labeled Shalimar.

A bright pink ribbon, tied into a blossom, was the only decoration on the otherwise unwrapped blue box.

"Oh, Doctor!" Awkwardly, she put down the coffee tray. And in a kind of idiotic confusion, she wiped her hands right on her bathrobe.

"Just a modest token of my regard for the wife of a dear friend."
He spoke almost in a whisper, as if the occasion required him to
remain standing with a serious and respectful expression on his
face . . . Valent was sickened by this feigned pathos, which his wife
was obviously incapable of perceiving. "No, no, Madam," he simply
continued, his voice now raised in intimate benevolence, "friendship is friendship, you understand, unconditionally, and it must be
nurtured."

Accepting the gift, she breathed out a lengthy "thank you," as if
thanking him mainly for the friendship.

"After all," he began, his eyes and voice indicating that he was
referring to the both of them, "we never know, do we? . . . Today
we're here, but tomorrow we could be gone . . ." As he spoke, he
steadied her cup, amiably and helpfully, so she would not spill the
coffee, then he saw to his own cup, politely said "thank you," and
breathing heavily, continued: "That's just the way it is; what can
you do? But for as long as we're here, we're here. I always say we're
a team, don't I, Vali? Nobody can live only for himself; he'll simply
go mad, I guess, or just collapse. I think that's the way we're made;
it's how we're defined . . ."

"As herds," Valent let out, although he hadn't intended to.

"As herds, if you like, but I would say, well, as teams."

His wife, of course, was nodding her head in agreement with the
"Doctor" as she took tiny sips of coffee, straightening her pinky
more markedly than usual. Then she remarked that teams are made
up of individuals.

"Exactly!" the "neighbor" broke in, seeming delighted. "An excellent point, Madam! Exactly! But consider this: every team pos-
sesses and is governed by something we call 'spirit'—'team spirit,'

we say. And this spirit is the thing we are all subject to, both as a group and individually. That applies to me, and to you too, Madam, and also to Vali."

"Spirit . . ." Pursing her lips, she gave it some thought.

"In the end I suppose it doesn't matter what we call it; we might even call it *demon* . . . yes . . . looking at the big picture, of course."

Valent watched him closely and felt afraid. Afraid of his every move . . . He couldn't take part in the conversation. He didn't even dare to consider throwing him out of the apartment. He could only suffer, agonize, ache—also because of this cursed fear that was choking him. He did manage to subdue it a little by assuming the guise of a worthy gentleman sitting in the comfort of his own home, who calmly smokes his pipe, despite the obviously strange way his wife was behaving, and who simply, as if he had no opinion on the matter, says nothing. Meanwhile, spinning in his head was the thought that his wife—and it could have only been her—must have told someone about his fantasy, his deception . . . regarding *Doctor Pavlovski*—"Mr." Mario, maybe? Or one of the women in the building? Or someone at the market?

"But why should . . . ?" he mumbled.

"Forgive me, Vali," the friendly "neighbor" casually interrupted. "I'll just take a moment to explain. About spirit, I mean . . . Yes, spirit is the thing that connects, or binds, individuals together." As he spoke, his fat eyes cast an ominous sidelong glance at Valent, which made him cringe, made his insides twist, and made his unasked question—Why would a "doctor" be wearing a cemetery uniform?—somehow stick in his throat.

"Yes, but . . ." Despite everything, he'd give it another try.

"Oh, Vali, please! You're . . ." Now it was his wife, scowling, who cut him off.

"That's just the way he is," the "neighbor" said, shrugging, a sign of amiable understanding, and the corners of his flabby mouth drew back. "Whether we like it or not. Well, now, about spirits . . . But let's leave spirits for another time. The coffee is superb, Madam, truly superb . . ." As if it had only now caught his attention, he picked up the ebony girl, at the same time throwing another quick glance at Valent.

"This . . ." For a brief second he adopted the appraising look of the connoisseur, then as if out of politeness put the statuette down again and said with a roguish smile, "This certainly does not belong on our team."

"That's Shulamite," his wife said, nodding, as if it were obvious, and took another sip of coffee.

Valent was plunged once more into blackness.

"Shulamite . . ." Sticking out his lower lip, the "neighbor" pondered the name. "How interesting . . ."

At this his wife, clearly, did not know whether she was supposed to laugh, or maybe only smile . . . but then somehow she realized he wasn't being funny.

"Vilma gave her to me." She scowled. "We were young." She addressed her explanation only to the "Doctor," as if she wanted to open her heart to him, at least a little. "Shulamite is Shulamite only when she is with her bridegroom and in love—that's what she told me, you know . . . and so on . . . But how is Mrs. Pavlovski?"

The "Doctor" was again turning the statuette in his hands, examining it more closely.

"There is no Mrs. Pavlovski," he sighed, with a kind of practiced resignation, without taking his eyes off the statuette.

"Oh, I see . . ." She regretted the question.

"No, no, Madam, it's quite all right."

In the silence that followed Valent might have said that he had had quite enough of this disgusting impertinence—but he didn't. He drew on his pipe and tried, in spite of it all, to behave as someone who commands the appropriate respect even when he says nothing. He did not recall his wife ever mentioning the name Shulamite in connection with the statuette, and this was surely the first he had ever heard of any Vilma—though of course this might not signify anything definite or useful, nor did it in any way ease the wretched tension he was feeling as the two of them went on chatting and his wife prattled away gracelessly, acting all sugary sweet as she showered attention on this allegedly unmarried "Doctor," their "neighbor." Nevertheless, he tried to follow what they were saying. Although they kept shifting away from him. And speaking more and more just between themselves. Even when they started talking about "Mr." Mario, whom, apparently, the "Doctor" knew—or so he claimed—"although Mario was, in a certain sense, always mysterious, a riddle even for those closest to him." To this, Valent might have added a thing or two, but it would have only annoyed them; they would have thought it inappropriate if he had said, for instance, that not only Mario, but each of us, is a mystery and a riddle unto himself . . . if they had bothered to listen, or would have even heard him, for his wife was wondering at this unexpected mutual acquaintance, to which the "Doctor" assured her that it was a small world and he knew Mario very well indeed. This, too, amazed his wife.

"A true eccentric, an adventurer," the "Doctor" observed. "And that was how he met his end . . ."

Now his wife, as if seeking an explanation, glanced at Valent, then back at the "neighbor," and only then asked, "What do you mean, 'met his end?'"

The "neighbor" said nothing, as if he wanted to take a few breaths in peace, and after a moment or so, as if unable to believe they did not know, he frowned.

"Yes, well . . . somebody cut his throat, you see . . ."

"But that's impossible!" She was dumbfounded.

Valent tried to act as if he hadn't been punched in the stomach. In this same posture, he also tried to withstand the "neighbor's" long and searching gaze, and with the thought in his mind that he might very possibly be sitting face to face with the Brežine police inspector, he told himself that, despite the man's cunning interrogation skills, he wouldn't let himself be dragged onto thin ice. The cemetery uniform might, of course, just be a ruse, but now he would have to be sharp, stay focused.

"But Vali, it was in the newspapers! You couldn't have missed it!" he insisted. The man was studying him, although now under the cover of being amazed at Valent's hardly credible ignorance.

Furrowing his brow, Valent did his best to take his pipe out of his mouth as calmly as possible, and then, swallowing hard, he asked, "So when did it happen?" He was absolutely certain that nothing bad had happened to "Mr." Mario, that the whole thing was maybe just some mix-up over names, or perhaps a fabrication—or a trap.

"You must tell us! Oh my, this is just so awful! What happened?" His wife shook her head and sighed. "It was his neck, you said?"

Valent was glad that she had pushed her way center stage, desperate for a share of their "neighbor's" attention.

"A surgical incision." He perhaps wished to have done with her quickly. For only a split second he took his eyes off Valent.

"What, so you've stopped reading the newspapers?" Again he was watching him. It sounded like a well-meaning, friendly reproof.

Valent decided to play along.

"You know how it is, at our age," he answered, as if indifferent, and even had his pipe between his teeth. He poured them all some cognac.

"But when did it happen? I mean . . ." His wife was curious.

"It's been a week or so, maybe a little more." The "neighbor" was making an effort to be pleasant.

"Such a nice man. He was rich . . ." She shook her head over the whims of fate. "I told you, Vali . . . He used to call us in the evening," she recalled, seeming to expect him to nod dutifully at her words for their "neighbor's" benefit. "I'd swear it under oath, I said . . ."

"There are firm suspicions. The police have a hot lead, they say."

Valent again tried to calmly endure the fat man's gaze.

"Oh, I do hope they catch him." She sighed, as if looking for at least a little consolation.

"But Vali, listen to me"—this time the "neighbor" preferred to ignore her histrionics—"The newspapers—well, okay. That, let's say, I can understand. But to neglect your old buddies, your friends—that, no. That I cannot permit. Certainly not now, when you and I are neighbors." Again he inhaled deeply.

"But we are all on the way down,"—Valent was struggling—"some of us one way; others, a different way. And when it's like that, all a person wants, more and more, is peace and quiet."

"Oh please! Did you hear what he said?" The man turned to Valent's wife, and as if speaking on her behalf too, continued: "You'll get plenty of peace and quiet soon enough, more than you bargained for. Nothing but peace and quiet for a long, long time . . ." He took a sip of cognac. Valent's wife showed that she agreed. "But as long as we're here"—as if grateful for her supportive nodding, he smiled at her—"we're here. That's the way it is, my dear Vali . . . As I always say, the spirit of friendship is what binds us together, and whether you want to or not, you have to give in to it." Now he was smiling at Vali too, but the goodwill was all on the surface; peering out from crescent-shaped folds of skin, his icy, menacing eyes contained no smile. On top of it all, his wife's fawning manner, her constant nodding, her barely concealed flirting with the "neighbor" was, more and more, provoking a maddeningly unpleasant feeling, as if her every gesture, her every smile and glance, was a fresh betrayal. It pained him that he didn't even have the courage to ask where this shameless "friendship" came from, and what was its point. He could even admit straight out that Doctor Pavlovski simply didn't exist—that is, he was merely a fabrication; nor were there any "old buddies," those high-class friends of his, and this lie he's been telling so many years, about meeting and socializing with them, was just his idiotic desire to appease his wife . . . But they would just look at him with scorn and repulsion, after which, very probably, the inspector would reach into his bulky pocket, pull out a badge, and direct and cold, start asking him supposedly routine questions, such as: so where did he go, then? Or: where was he on such-and-such a day at such-and-such a time? . . . And the skein would start to unwind. And his wife wouldn't hesitate to mention— for the record—every single time he hadn't been at home. And somehow, somewhere, in the middle of the investigation, a scalpel would turn up . . . So by all means he had to keep his cool, even while the "neighbor," leaning much too close and breathing heavily, told his wife about the circumstances surrounding the murder of "Mr." Mario; how they found his naked, perfumed body with a precise, clean incision across the jugular artery; he also mentioned black opals—everything was identical, in short, to what Valent had read about the Brežine murder.

"It was the heirs," she surmised, nodding knowledgeably. "Had to be them." He said he didn't know, shrugging; so far, at least, no one had come forward to claim the inheritance. Apparently, he was not particularly interested in her surmising, even though he seemed to be looking at her at the same time with a covert, silent vow, which did not escape Valent, who more than anything else saw it as just another one of the inspector's tricks by which he was probably trying to get a witness on his side.

"But that's why they're not coming forward," she persisted in her theory. "They're in hiding."

"Excellent! That must be it, dear lady!" He feigned enthusiasm. "That's it exactly! What intuition! No mistake about it: intuition! What are your thoughts, Vali?"

"You'll see"—she was positively glowing, now confident—"an innocent heir will be found . . ."

"Madam, you're incredible! You truly are! I tell you, in all sincerity," he said, unconvincingly, "you've done a first-rate job working it out!" She did not pick up on the act. Valent, meanwhile, felt his stomach convulse: in this false enthusiasm too, he saw the inspector's method, a way to shake, to crack, the suspect's patient composure, to make him jittery, impatient, and then, maybe out of the blue, at exactly the right time, in exactly the right way, he would strike . . .

In such a case, a quick and well-executed retreat seemed the best plan. True, it wouldn't be easy; he mustn't do anything to arouse further suspicion. But of course, even an overly obliging patience might arouse suspicion. So he gave himself the task of cleaning his pipe and made an effort to take part in the conversation, but only with a certain insouciance, while at the same time acting at least a little aloof. He felt the other man's eyes sizing him up, coldly assessing the situation, gathering an impression and devising a suitable plan of attack, maybe a particular method as well, some tried-and-true approach that wouldn't let up, that would be impossible to deter. It was difficult to curb or suppress his nervous uncertainty, the belief that the inspector had already made up his mind and wasn't really interested in actual guilt. He simply wanted and needed to have a guilty party. And so he'd made his choice . . .

"When was the last time you went out?" he began again, clucking his tongue, as if he were asking mainly out of friendly concern.

"I go out occasionally," Valent shrugged, nodding, a few moments later yawning to fill the unexpected silence that had followed.

"You go out occasionally," the other man snorted, with a note of reproach, and again fell silent. Now not even from Valent's wife did he try to conceal his probing gaze, his probing superiority—as if he simply had the right.

"I've got something for you, too." Maybe he had paused before saying this just so the words would resonate with greater meaning. Now he pulled an ordinary door key from his pocket and placed it on the table in front of Valent. "I want you to have it," he added.

"What's this?" Valent asked.

"It's friendship, Vali." He smiled at him with his cold, round eyes. Then, turning to Valent's wife, he explained that he traveled a lot, that he was away more often than not, and that he would be most grateful if Vali might look in on the apartment from time to time. Valent, meanwhile, had pushed the key away, which seemed to him an expressive enough refusal to do any sort of "looking in" on the apartment.

"Vali, I really need you to do this for me"—he spoke earnestly, with a twitch in his cheeks—"for various reasons, you know, and there are the lilies . . . You know, I raise lilies, Madam," he explained to Valent's wife, "and if a man is by himself . . . I have three now, and they're just about to bloom . . . Well, what can I say? They're my darlings."

From her expression, it was evident she wanted to volunteer to do the favor herself. Valent hoped she really would. But she must have reconsidered. She lowered her eyes. In visible embarrassment. Maybe she was waiting to be asked . . . but of course he was no more interested in her than he was in his lilies—he was plotting something else entirely, and he obviously didn't fail to notice Valent's perplexity and nervous tension and fearfulness and anxiety, which had again rendered him incapable of thinking about the position he was in with any clarity whatsoever. Now his wife had pushed the key back in front of him. And with palpable woundedness in her voice, speaking on his—Valent's—behalf, she promised the "neighbor" everything—that he would take care of the apartment, and water the lilies, and everything would be the way it should be.

"If I'm asking too much . . ."—the "neighbor," disingenuously, started backtracking—"Vali, if it's at all inconvenient for you . . ." Then he stopped. And waited. Meanwhile, his wife insisted that something like that could hardly be any trouble or inconvenience for Vali. And still he was silent. Waiting. While Valent feverishly tried to determine if maybe now was the moment to step out of this deception, abandon this charade—to come clean, in other words, and simply admit what he would probably, one way or the other, eventually be forced to admit . . .

"So when, then?" was, from all of this, the only thing he managed to choke out.

"What?" the neighbor frowned, all the folds in his face gathered into what seemed an expression of offense, and without waiting for an answer, continued with a note of despair in his voice: "Listen, Vali, if it's too much trouble, or if you can't, or maybe don't want to, just say so. I'm only asking. I'm new here. I thought I could count on you, because I'm leaving tomorrow, at daybreak. That's all." Even as he was saying this, breathing heavily, he stood up. As if he really were offended. "Madam, please do forgive me if I've disturbed you." In spite of it all, he had no wish to slight the "lady of the house." He didn't even look back at them as he left. Valent's wife tottered after him.

The key remained on the table.

15

Afterwards, on several successive nights, he heard muffled girlish noises. The sound of sobbing, or sometimes singing, or sometimes a gaspy whimpering . . . Muffled, most often hardly audible, it stole into his hearing—mostly through the wall, from Kremavc's (the "neighbor's") apartment, but also now and then it seemed to come from behind the door, or from behind a cabinet, or somewhere close by, so that he looked around in alarm even as he doubted he had heard anything, and was filled with that kind of fear that makes your chest tremble and your cheeks burn in anticipation. And all of it together, at the same time, is also remorse. Periods of silence dragged inbetween. For whole hours, even, nothing unusual could be heard. But then it would start up again. It would even wake him up. And he would get out of bed. And walk around the apartment as if deranged until daybreak when the "mountain" began to rise, though these days he thought it looked a little strangely bloated with a deathly bluish hue. In some places a kind of cherry tinge might glimmer through, but it would soon expire, go out, unable to ripen into dawn and the sun . . . and the sun itself seemed to take longer to rise, and when it did, was like a heavy, tawny honeybread cookie. Heaviness remained throughout the day, as well as a kind of anxious and oppressive feeling of guilt, as if he'd had a shamefully sordid romp with some whorish creature. In vain he told himself that nothing of the sort had happened, that although he had taken the so-called neighbor's key from the cabinet, several times in fact, he had always put it back again, because his thoughts squirmed through his head like worms, conveying only revulsion, remorse, and the kind of aversion he used to feel years ago when he would return home feeling empty, save for his agonizing self-contempt, from bought women. A feeling of hollow tension filled his stomach now, and his conscience felt cold, slimy, and as though about to cave in on itself . . . while his wife was asking if he had watered, or when was he going to water, those lilies, which must certainly be very rare and valuable, since that sort of "Doctor" wouldn't be raising ordinary lilies, which, anyway, certainly wouldn't be in bloom at this time of year. And besides, when a person makes a promise . . .

"I didn't promise anything." He wanted to put an end to the matter.

"What do you mean, you didn't promise anything?" She was astonished, for she had been right there herself; she had heard him. "A man puts his trust in you, gives you his key . . ." She wouldn't let it go; she couldn't understand why it was so hard for him to go next door and do a favor for someone.

What he wanted to do most was shut himself away somewhere. To hide. Hide, too, from that thing in his head that was after him . . . that was like a little girl with azure eyes. To hide and not have to hear that such a "Doctor" deserves respect; and not to have to keep quiet about the fact that *this* "Doctor" is not actually the *real* "Doctor," because the *real* "Doctor" is just someone he had thought up.

"I don't know why you're staring at me so idiotically," she said. He himself didn't know why either, actually. He also didn't know that his staring was idiotic. It had never occurred to him that staring at her well-lotioned but nonetheless wrinkled neck could even be idiotic. By all means, from now on he would try to stare at her intelligently. But in spite of this, she fumed at him, the vein in her neck nearly popping, and told him she was fed up, had had enough, was about to go crazy . . . All he wanted to do was hide. And he felt that somewhere there existed, for him alone, a honey-yellow room, and that on the floor of this otherwise empty room, there lay, not some bristly rug, a boarskin maybe, or a bearskin, but something else—maybe, indeed, something resembling the skin of a bear or a boar, though definitely not such a skin—something that wraps a person tight . . .

He couldn't speak to her about it.

Yet he didn't know what he could say or perhaps even understand—nevertheless, it seemed, and appeared, and also meant, that it was hardly sufficient if *he* knew nothing about it, if *he* didn't understand; that not knowing, not understanding, didn't suffice—and that any knowledge whatsoever about anything, any understanding whatsoever about anything, was extremely meager and unreliable.

He could, it's true, have simply said that it had to do with some doormat; he could even tell his wife that, whatever was necessary, and then cover his tracks later.

"The lilies are just the doormat," he said out loud, maybe too fast, although initially he wasn't thinking of lilies. "What's the point of watering someone's doormat?" he persisted, despite the unpleasant feeling that he was probably getting ahead of himself. He peered even more intelligently at the vein in his wife's neck. "So tell me, what's the point?" he demanded, as if to reproach her for all that earlier silliness over a few lilies. Maybe he would have kept on tearing into her and her astonished grimace, had he not suddenly seen *her*—splendid, slightly translucent, slightly honeyed, with opals around her neck, she was leaning against the window and, completely indifferent and bored, was letting her gaze wander across the eastern districts.

"That thing is a bed," she may even have said . . . as if his wife's presence made no difference to her . . . she may have said it right to the window . . . and also may have added that beds have to be watered—much more softly, as if hinting at something.

Amazingly, his wife paid no attention to her. Perhaps she wanted to show that she knew how to preserve her womanly dignity, her womanly pride—and she couldn't see that the honeyed degenerate by the window was aware of her own superiority and advantage, and that honey was slowly dripping from the blade of the scalpel she held in her hand.

"Why can't you see that I'm all yours, and yours alone?" she sighed reproachfully, as if her heart was aching. And stepped away from the window. He bowed his head. He should probably warn his wife. But he didn't. He said nothing. He was unable to and didn't want to at the same time . . . He felt a shudder. He felt guilty . . . Although the girl, clenching the scalpel tightly in her fist, didn't then move toward his wife, who obviously sensed nothing as she said that she would make a phone call; she'd see to it that he was put where he belonged. The girl took the key out of the glass cabinet. And waited for their eyes to meet. Her azure gaze filled his breast with sweetness and tenderness and embraced his heart.

Then she returned the key and left.

His heart, his breast, trembled with joy. And his wife didn't understand why he smiled at her then; why he then—despite her resistance and refusal—still wanted to caress her and embrace her; why he sat down in the armchair and then stood right up again and didn't know what to do with himself; and everything seemed delightful to him, even when he told her softly that he felt wonderful, that his heart was filled with warmth, that he would do everything she wanted, that he would go right now to water the lilies, that she shouldn't worry about a thing . . . she didn't understand. You could see it in her eyes, which looked frightened. It was evident in her drawn face, her clenched lips; even the vein in her neck pulsated excitedly, rapidly, and he thought she would start screaming if he tried to caress her again.

He didn't try.

Instead, for no special reason, he went into the bedroom and stood by the window, looking out over the rooftops and chimneys. He tried to breathe out the urge to laugh from the pit of his stomach and that awful bit of uncertainty that had lodged itself firmly in his mind, stirring up doubts, such as whether he had really and truly seen her, and whether he had really and truly understood, and whether he had really been given permission to . . . she could have just been coquettishly amusing herself, making fun of him, or she could be part of some vile deceit in cahoots with the "neighbor," some "investigation"—they might even accuse him of sexually harassing, or even abusing, a minor. All that. All that . . . but he definitely wanted to spruce himself up, change his clothes, and make an impression.

The best thing would be, it seemed to him, to leave as if he were going to Brežine. To again tell his wife the old white lie about that group of doctors and professors. And that he would (he'd add in a whisper) stop by that fellow Pavlovski's place on the way out and water those lilies, because maybe he really ought to do him this favor, although of course he didn't want to because something can always go wrong in another person's apartment. Which leads to a lot of bother and responsibility, and in the end you get more resentment than gratitude for your trouble.

This time he applied a little extra complexion cream to his tired and wrinkled face. True, he wasn't very happy with it; true, every facial expression he tried to practice for *her* proved a dismal fiasco in the mirror; but it would have been even worse without the cream. His sparse yellow teeth seemed to him to be yellower and sparser than ever before. And his gray hair was lifeless. His nose was ridiculously pointy; his chin was too short and it rounded off too soon. Set within swollen, purplish circles, his rheumy eyes were weak and vague; and his pale—in spots even bluish—lips hardly seemed capable of puckering up into anything like a kiss. He told himself he was being childish. But it didn't help. Also, the cream was getting on his nerves. But without it, one saw the little veins, the spots, the pores—all his naked misery . . . He did, however, regain a little self-confidence from his impeccable Brežine evening suit, which, with his ring and the gold stickpin in his necktie, gave even his hair, even his nose and his chin a veneer of high-class distinction.

His wife didn't ask where he was going. Only now and then, as he was walking into the bathroom, or the bedroom, or the front hall, did he catch her covert glances, which she quickly withdrew each time. Later too, when, fully dressed and groomed, he was simply sitting in his chair, or tamping and drawing on his pipe, or pouring himself a cognac, and trying to smile sweetly at all of this, she kept looking at him in the same way.

From time to time he listened to the TV a little—there was happiness and sadness and a certain pain and overwrought screaming; somebody shot somebody or at least wanted to; then there was fighting, and again, laughing . . . and all the while *she* was there in the Kremavc apartment, walking back and forth, waiting, and probably looking at the door . . . But nevertheless, he waited patiently until the whole sky was completely dark. And restlessly hoped and kept repeating to himself that everything would be fine . . . At last, however, suddenly and determinedly, he stood up, put his pipe and smoking gear in his pocket, and took the key. But at that very moment, a woman's voice from the television cried out accusingly, as if in pain: "Oh, oh, oh . . . !" So despite his earlier determination, he stood there for another moment or two. Waiting. For the voices to get brighter. But right then someone said: "She's dead . . ." Which certainly couldn't be a good omen. Which is why he poured himself another cognac and drank it and looked at his watch and walked over to the window . . . It was not until the people on television were playing and shouting again and, from what he could tell, dancing, that he turned around quickly and, without a single word, dashed out of the apartment.

He hadn't expected the lights in the hallway to be on.

Also, the elevator was humming, but luckily, it was going to one of the floors above.

He was worried about the Marzis. Who might still be on the lookout for him. So he stood in front of his door for a bit. Like someone who, just because he happens to feel like it, steps outside his apartment and takes a look around . . . The elevator stopped maybe two or three floors above. And stayed there. And was silent.

The doors to the apartments on the left and right were, as far as he could see, closed. But, his head throbbing, he had to tell himself quite a few more times that everything would be fine, everything would be fine . . . before walking over, before pushing down the handle of the "neighbor's" door. Which was locked. The nameplate with the inscription "Gustav Kremavc, retiree" was still there. And he had to rummage through his pockets, through his smoking gear, to get the key.

As he was doing this, somewhere further down the hallway he thought he heard a door shut very softly. He didn't look around. He just unlocked the door and stepped inside. And locked it again.

There was a smell.

Shalimar . . .

It was dark.

Through the open door of the front hall, it was, indeed, possible to see some of the city's glow through the window on the opposite wall. But his eyes still had to adjust . . . He had no difficulty, however, with the light switch; he found it immediately right next to the door-jamb. The many light bulbs in the living room chandelier reminded him of candles. A few garments, apparently Kremavc's, still hung in the front hall wardrobe. And there was a pair of men's shoes lying in front of the doorway that looked as though someone in a hurry had just kicked them off. There were also some freshly planed boards leaning against the wall in the living room. And a hammer was lying on the floor in a corner. And it flashed through his mind that such boards could be used to make a coffin . . . But at the same time his attention was drawn to the nude pictures hanging on the wall. Several were actual paintings and were framed, but most of them had been cut out of cheap, sometimes pornographic, magazines. He said: "Good evening." And listened. And waited a little. As his suspicion that there was nobody in the apartment grew, so did his disappointment. It looked deserted. Old Kremavc himself might even have left it this way. Timber and all. Dried stains could be seen on the tablecloth in the dining nook. The unwashed plate in the sink was covered in mold. The bedroom was the same way. Covered in dust, airless. With old dirty bed linen. Over the headboard hung a picture of three lilies in bloom on a reddish dark background.

Mingled with the dankness, the smell of Shalimar, especially in the bedroom, was sickeningly sweet.

A kind of sorrow took hold of him, as if for everything that had happened. It was painful. He was ashamed of having had such hopes, of having been tricked like this. Again he was overcome by fear, by that deep and bitter disillusionment against which it was no longer possible to act. But when he, will-less and dejected, opened the door to the bathroom, indifferently and without really thinking about it, he froze. In horror. In shock.

A body lay there.

A girl.

With a large towel spread beneath her.

Slightly splayed.

With one leg bent seductively . . . and she was smiling. Although her eyes were closed. And she was obviously trying to stay like that, as if asleep, as if innocent . . . her smooth, arched belly rose and fell excitedly, and this same excitement was visible, too, in her breasts, which, though not fully matured, were still adorably grown, adorably protruding. The downy, endearingly cheek-like little furrow between her legs formed a chocolate-colored pout as if in a kiss . . . maybe just that—just a kiss, he thought, maybe just warm breath, kneeling down, bending over her, touching her gently with his lips, without a word, eyes closed . . . as if pursuing the shyly receding dream in her barely budding flowerlike core . . . She did not stir. And he could only stand there gazing at her. And trembling in deep fear, because it must not, simply could not last, because maybe he would already be on his knees, except he still didn't know if she would let him . . .

"Why are you only looking at me?" she whispered, but as if in agony, as if ill . . .

"You're beautiful," he stammered, his lips dry, and was almost startled by his own voice, which seemed not in the least suitable . . . He wanted to correct the impression right away, so with barely restrained haste he staggered forward and crouched down and leaned over her face.

"You're beautiful . . ." he repeated, whispering, as if needing to console her. She didn't open her eyes. As if worn out, she was still trying to show something like a smile. He didn't know what else to say. He didn't know where to touch her so it wouldn't be terrible and frustrating for them both. But then she herself took his hand. And placed it on her neck.

He felt her necklace.

A sticky liquid.

Blood. It trickled . . . from a wound cut in an arc from behind the ear to below the chin . . . it dripped into his hand. As from a flame. Black and whirling, it whacked him. He could hardly keep from falling over. Maybe he screamed, or gaped silently, but it definitely skewered him, he definitely felt a sense of horror, and the corner of the towel was in his hands, and confused frenzy and confused despair, as he tried to stop the blood, but soon it was seeping through the bunched-up towel and his fingers, and the girl wanted something, maybe to tell him something, maybe to show him something, maybe to take his arm, to lift herself up. But she fell back limp. Her eyes opened wide. Her head jerked to the side, her neck bent strangely. And she stayed like that. With her neck strangely bent, her eyes open wide. Her mouth gaping. Her arms drooped lifelessly as he shook her, pressed her to his chest, squeezed her in his arms . . . and as he kept sitting there, in a tepid, sticky puddle of blood.

16

He didn't know when or how he had sneaked out of the apartment tower. His heart was racing. He was short of breath. There was tightness in his chest. His head was aching. He didn't know. He couldn't understand. There was a quivering in his stomach. That was all he knew. Nothing else. He just stood there like that. In front of the building. It wouldn't go away. But even so he just stood there and looked around and there was a convulsion in his belly as if he was about to laugh.

There was a hum from the neighboring streets. People, too, were walking along these streets; he could see them, but they were too far away, too removed, although they too were causing that burning feeling, as if from a red-hot spear. In his heart.

Monster! they would say—or nothing; this was pecking at him.

Should somebody happen to come by, he would tell the person—would explain, would confess—that this is how they set people up—that's what he'd say—they set people up, they set them up; they set them up because of the newspapers, the television—and then there would again be one less reprobate at large.

But for a long time nobody came by.

The apartment tower was silent, as if deserted. The windows above the front steps showed only darkness. And it seemed to him that the building was alien, dead; that it was no longer his home.

He was shivering, as if from coldness, from fever, from both at once, and his fingers were annoyingly sticky, but still he was sure he would be able to do it, to step out of the shadows, that is, to stand in front of whoever passes by and tell him, confide to him, convince him . . .

The two girls whom he presumed to be students passed by.

Wearing heels that were too high, skirts that were too short, in garish makeup and wagging their hips, they were walking toward him. And didn't notice him. His courage faltered. He could not step forward. Call out after them. Nor did he know how to start, what to say . . .

Instead he retreated behind a corner of the building.

After which, despite his heart, despite his shortness of breath, despite everything, he wanted to flee.

Get away.

Anywhere.

Although there were people walking everywhere, driving everywhere, getting in and out of vehicles . . . people with soulless, leaden faces.

There were probably maintenance men and security guards waiting in vestibules, who probably would not want, not be able to understand that he hadn't been able to help it, hadn't been able to do anything, that she had wanted something, with her neck strangely bent, had been trying to do something, but didn't have the strength . . . Even if he had screamed. Yes, that. Exactly that. And it would have meant sadness, despair, *her* lying there limp, dead, with her unseeing eyes opened wide, with that absence, which you gaze over and then slink away, and no longer know, no longer understand, and mostly just want to hide.

Nobody cared that he was staggering around as if drunk, stopping, leaning against a wall, trying to avoid the glow of lights and trying to fight off the thought that was lashing, lashing at him and like a sharp whip spurring his heart, spurring his steps onward, past this corner, past that corner, from street to street, somewhere, anywhere, maybe toward the embankment, or maybe not, somewhere across the streetcar tracks, through an intersection and a square, as if through alien, unknown territory, through a passageway with graffiti, and again along a street, an avenue, past some meager, sparse shrubbery . . . From behind which appeared a big black car with honey-yellow lights, driving slowly, as if looking for someone. He wanted to hide. But he didn't have time. Through the car's tinted windows, a few leaden expressions were visible. They drove slowly, too slowly. Past him. And turned. At the first intersection. He too would have turned there—the embankment could be in that direction. But now he would have to go a different way. Go somewhere else. They could be waiting. Their faces dead. And it occurred to him that sometimes the sun shone like that, with a dead light, and that for people all this was, for as long as it lasted, merely the play of honey-yellow images. After they drove away, after they turned the corner, he did his best to act at least a little more like somebody out on a stroll. To slow his pace. To lift his head. And straightening his spine, with his hands behind his back, simply to walk, simply to believe that he was not the one who had cut her throat, that he was not the one who had tossed the scalpel away. And simply to consider that somewhere there was a certain lady who would again utter the word *phantom*. But it didn't work. It didn't help. A bleeding, aching void gaped in him, and not far off, in front of a florist's brightly illuminated shop window, there suddenly loomed the corpulent figure of a man. He avoided it. He crossed to the other, more shadowy side of the street. Kept close to the wall. And sensed him watching. And from the corner of his eye noticed that there were funeral wreaths hanging in that brightly lit window.

The man's eyes followed him.

A heavy, tawny gaze that hobbled his step, stiffened his torso, and caused the curved pattern in the cobblestones to fluctuate.

Even after he turned a corner.

Later too.

When who knows how many streets away, out of breath, he eventually stopped. And collapsed on a step behind a low little wall between two columns. And from there listened in terror. To the street.

To the footsteps.

Which approached individually or mixed with those of others. And receded. Which, resonant or muted, shuffled and minced along and got lost in or became separate from the others and from the distant background hum. And kept on coming and coming. As if lost. As if not knowing where to go . . . He was most afraid of steps that were slow, soft and heavy. Each time he expected them to suddenly stop. To be heading towards him. To be coming for him. He expected a gray, leaden expression to appear over the little wall . . . and it didn't let up, as he shivered there, exhausted and freezing.

Not even when the light of the streetlights started fading slowly into the pale, purplish morning.

Night started dwindling away just a little too fast . . .

But in the pale morning light he saw with amazement that in fact there was no blood on his hands.

None at all. Not even a little.

He couldn't find a single spot of blood.

Nor was there anything sticky anywhere.

Again and again, he turned his hands in the light . . . There was no blood on his suit either, although otherwise it was rumpled and ruined.

It was as if it had simply gone away. Evaporated.

Not even the soles of his shoes had any blood on them.

There was not a spot, not a trace, on the step or on the little wall, nothing sticky, slimy, or clotted; even when it was fully day and most of the people passing by were hurrying importantly to their jobs; even when he took off his jacket, when across the street he found a window display with a background mirror and examined himself thoroughly once again—even then he found nothing that could have ever been blood.

Nothing.

Even though in the window display in front of him women's clothes in stylish shades of violet and burgundy with green, black, blue, or white accessories and accents were draped on stands and mannequins; even though the street was the street and the passers-by were passing by . . . There was nothing. Not on his pants, or his jacket, or his shirt, or under his fingernails. Nothing. Even though he remembered being stunned, bewildered, frantic, remembered how he had to get away as fast as possible, get out of the bathroom, out of the apartment; how he had then locked the door, how he had sat in that spreading black puddle as she lay bleeding, lifeless in his arms . . . and still lingered in his mind relentlessly. As did the anguish. And the despair. And it was impossible to think differently.

He walked on a few paces and examined himself again in the next shop window.

And again he couldn't believe it.

It was as if a dark whirlwind was starting to blow—and he had to do something, anything, right away, right away . . . to stop the woman who was just now approaching and ask her, standing in front of her with his arms up over his head, his palms facing out—is there any blood anywhere? He moaned, he pleaded . . .

She was frightened.

She gasped sharply.

He tried to be friendlier, more polite, and also with his arms, he tried putting them like this, a little lower . . .

But she jumped away.

In shock, with a look of dismay on her face.

And darted past him, into the crowd, toward a traffic intersection with streetcars that could be seen above the heads and bodies coming and going . . . He wanted to explain, to apologize. But he took only two steps after her. It hit him like a cold and icy splash. Stopped him in his tracks. Seared him. And everyone walking this way and that way was acting the same, was similarly silent. And would have jumped away if he stretched out his hands . . . even if he clasped them together, if he fell on his knees, they would jump away just as she did, would step away, and each and every time there would be a splash—a wordless, outwardly casual command visible in their shallow eyes, their leaden expressions . . . and from the honey-hazy grayness above the street.

Go away, they demanded, their eyes on the ground or the shop windows, on a distant intersection or into the honey-grayness . . . Go away, their silence said, their walking said, when he turned to follow one or another of them and no longer lifted his arms and no longer dared ask them anything.

Had he been at home, he would have been waiting at the window and consulting the "mountain." About everything. Even about his suit. Even about this or that lawyer from his appointment book . . . But he was not at home, and between the buildings, and across the intersection, there was no "mountain" to be seen; neither to the left nor to the right along the street, nor above the heads, nor among the passers-by, was there any "mountain"; not in people's eyes, or in the shop windows, or on the big billboard a little further down, in which a reclining, naked, honey-sweet image of a girl was, like some goddess of the streets, flashing a smile.

17

He did not belong with them, at the streetcar stop, on the streetcar . . . They were pale, as if still cold, as if they had just now come to life, jostling and pushing—and cold slithered from their eyes, snake-like, all over him. The streetcar smelled of various colognes and perfumes, of cheap hair gels, and beneath it all, the rankness of airless bedrooms. Mainly, however, he spent the ride staring out the window. And in spite of everything, in spite of his growing fatigue and his clothes, which were getting looks from people, he tried to act as if he were one of them.

He also exited the streetcar as if he were one of them.

They were rushing to work . . . while he did not know where he was going.

An hour, perhaps, went by, maybe more, as he stood at the streetcar stop with pain in his legs, a persistent pecking in his heart, at times feeling quite dazed, not knowing where he was or where he wanted to go, and nevertheless, like the others, kept looking to see if a streetcar was coming, and checking his watch, as if worried about being late for something. He had no desire to deal with the morning crowds on the streetcars and the roads.

In the meantime, honey-like and heavy, the sun had crept above the rooftops.

And when increasingly emptier streetcars started stopping at the increasingly emptier streetcar stop, he had to move on, go somewhere else.

Now it was a little more comfortable on the streetcar—nobody was leaning against him or banging into him as he peered drowsily through the glass at the passing succession of façades and streets and roads, and tried to forget the previous night, tried to find at least some consolation, at least some hope, in the thought that, even so, maybe they would soon find the real perpetrator, the real *monster*, that it would all be fine, it would all be fine . . . Even the thought that he might just go back home crossed his mind. But they would ambush him—the inspector, reporters, Oletič, the Marzis, his wife . . . and they'd probably push him around, roughen him up, put him in handcuffs; it'd be no good fighting back, no good shouting, pleading, explaining, no good pointing a finger at the inspector—and the newspapers and TV stations would run pictures of "The monster from the 15th floor," "The villain at the scene of the crime" . . . He broke out in a sweat just thinking about it; he felt sharp pains in his belly, tightness in his chest, over and over again . . . and there was no help for it. He had to get away. To go off somewhere again. And get on again. And stay seated by the window. And wait. And keep on gazing, gazing out . . . for behind his tired eyelids, which were getting heavier and heavier, the night lingered on, mercilessly, and there was still, mercilessly, the mute and motionless corpse of a girl.

As the steamy morning drew on, the crowds of people pushing and shoving were mainly pensioners: youthfully dressed, perfumed old ladies in too-short skirts; old men in youthful attire, whether casual or for the office—and they were all, with their briefcases and market baskets and purses, hurrying about on "errands."

With them, too, he got off somewhere. But then once more, pursued by covert glances, he took refuge behind a dirty streetcar window, which crawled past fleeting outlines, past gleaming rows of cars in traffic jams, past brief moments, close up, far away, as his tired eyes could barely stay open and everything was twisting lazily away; like some phantom of the night, a hearse made a slow turn through an intersection; a poisonously green-and-red building caught his eye; somewhere else, a snow-white statue of a girl with a pitcher crept by and slowly sank, passed, like one thing or another, into a steamy, weary torpor, into a vast and drowsy darkness . . . where she was lying, where she was waiting, with her eyes wide open. Extinguished. Without a god. Hah. And as if to soothe him, a thought—or maybe a dream—came to him: that she would be taken away and placed in those mornings, those glorious mornings . . . The door—it was only the door—hissed and rattled. He also caught the eyes of a few people. Who quickly looked away. And he told himself that he had to keep on the lookout, to wait for a stop, and to think about streets, about the day . . . from one place and another, as if invisible, the god of the street taunted him and the shimmeringly hot haze was like a heavy yellowed pall across faces, across the building façades and the commotion and the people rushing back and forth, across walls and windows, the all-too-often-empty windows, the all-too-often-broken windows, and the seemingly pointless rows of columns . . . and also across the long and much-too-congested four-lane road with apartment towers on either side, and also across a woman dressed in mourning who appeared from who knows where and was standing next to him . . .

With a pale face.

She had probably been crying not long before.

Which made him stand up, almost jumping out of his seat. And only then, as if out of consideration, politeness, did he manage to stammer out: "Please sit down." And he didn't look at her again as he hurried, as he pushed his way to the door and, as if pressed for time and terribly late, was one of the first to exit.

It was only when he was standing at the streetcar stop that it seemed to him that she had been looking at him condescendingly, with pitying eyes . . . and that everyone who had exited after him had been particularly silent and had dispersed with particular haste.

Partly from this, and partly from an increasingly unpleasant sense of isolation in this remote corner of the city, there was a nervous quivering in his stomach and throughout his tired limbs, while along the too-narrow four-lane road, cars and trucks of all sizes, one after the other without hardly any interruption, came roaring up and roaring past, horribly close by, wheezing and rumbling—everything but a streetcar.

Across the road there stood another lonely streetcar stop, which so far had remained deserted.

Heat vapor was rising off the blistering asphalt, off the plaza in front of the nearby yellow towers. And above the roadway, over the passing traffic, the air shimmered vilely in a yellowish haze.

Even so, he tried to wait with sufficient composure, sufficient patience.

And tried to spot a streetcar among the shimmering rows of trucks and cars.

But he couldn't help noticing through the haze, about a hundred yards back or so, what appeared to be a brick wall running along the opposite side of the road. Little columns, too . . . and at about mid-height of the wall and columns, there was a barely visible series of patina green swirls, most likely meant to represent waves. The towers in the surrounding area seemed to stand at a respectful distance. So it was a cemetery, he thought with a shrug. One of many. Nothing important. Nothing special. Peace and tranquility. Silence. Naturally, it was better to think about something else. Even if only about the streetcar—which was nowhere to be seen in either direction—and again his thoughts drifted toward something about chimneys, and crematoria, and hardly-ever-noticeable puffs of smoke, and hardly-ever-noticeable lonelinesses and those silences that followed, of which, most likely, the god of the street was not master. There were no streetcars coming . . . He also looked for taxicabs, but to no avail. It was mostly just a lot of trucks rumbling by in both directions.

And coming from that same wall a figure appeared . . . It disappeared briefly behind the trucks, but then it was coming his way, getting closer, moving pensively somehow, or maybe just lazily because of the steamy heat and the thick, muggy air, which was impossible to breathe without a struggle. The rather ample figure of a man . . . with a white shirt beneath a grayish-brown jacket that was carelessly buttoned across his belly. The pants, too, were grayish-brown.

He was in no hurry. He didn't look around. It was as if he were just walking, his head bowed as if carrying a burden across the back of his neck. And even from the other side of the road, it was possible to see in his whole appearance a certain lazy, egotistically shameless arrogance . . .

He stopped at the opposite streetcar stop.

And didn't look to see if a streetcar was coming, at least not right away.

The features of his face were impossible to make out.

Then, his head still bowed, he started rocking gently back and forth, with his hands in his pants pockets; it was as if, with his eyes on the ground and not paying attention to anything else, he was amusing himself with this shifting of weight from toe to heel and back again. And only after a while, as if it was a real bother to do so, did he look across the road.

And he didn't look away.

Valent, certainly, tried to be nonchalant; he even turned away and made an effort to think about the streetcar. But it wasn't working. There was no streetcar. There was nobody else at the stop. And before too long, that gaze was making him woozy, giving him chills. Again he felt that quivering. Like a clenching around his heart . . . and he knew he had to get away. At once. That he might even have to make a run for it now. But at that moment all he could muster was an awkward stagger, and only eventually did he somehow find his stride, regretting having gone down the sidewalk instead of heading immediately for the plaza and making his way between the towers . . . His heart was pounding wildly, erratically, in his skull and in his ears. "Keep going," he said, trying to steady himself. "Just keep walking. Who cares about anything else."

And right there, only a short distance from the streetcar stop and the plaza in front of the towers, was a steep concrete slope. He should have turned around, but he kept on walking nevertheless, trying to keep himself erect and not daring to turn his head. "Keep going," he told himself again, over and over—there's no going back . . . each time the phrase just attached itself to him, as of its own accord, like those tuneless, persistent jingles that sometimes got stuck in his head and wouldn't go away. Horribly, hypnotically. "Keep going." There's no going back.

But then he did look around, quickly, and saw, for the most part, trucks.

He looked a second time and it was exactly the same—nobody on the sidewalk—and the chilly tightness eased up a bit; things were still spinning as though he was at the edge of some enormous and shadowy chasm, but now it was starting to feel more like being a little too drunk, when you're chilled straight through but nonetheless manage a kind of smile, and without any clear plan, your lips curve a little, you wave it all away, shake your head, and tell yourself to keep on going; and the refrain repeats, it's almost a kind of comfort, that there's no going back.

He looked around a few more times, just to be sure. And with a kind of contempt, too, with scorn, and suddenly decided that, given the possibility of similar unwelcome encounters, he had best get rid of his identification. Right away he pulled it out of his pocket. *Valent Kosmina*—yes, the face in the photo, stupidly staring and twisted into a sort of grin; yes, and numbers—it had always seemed imbecilic to him, this staring, this grinning on identification documents. That was also why, without thinking twice, he tore his ID paper in half. Tore through the imbecility, the numbers. And tore it again. Into smaller pieces. Tiny little pieces. Which he crumpled in his fist. And threw beneath the wheels of the passing traffic. And as a kind of comfort said in their wake, "Keep going . . ." Hah. The tiny pieces whirled around and flew into the air and scattered behind a truck. And something else, too, got twisted into the thought that there was no going back, something about all these names whirling around everywhere, carried in all directions, while people, on the other hand, kept going, kept moving in one and the same direction . . . Several such names were luridly offering themselves from the graffiti on the concrete slope next to the sidewalk—powerlessness, despair maybe, religion, and again and again, provocatively accentuated genitalia, naked bodies, ominous, lustful, demon-like faces—the faces of terror, maybe, or of a god . . . "Keep going," would have been his contribution to all this, what he would have written there.

It was only after some time had passed that, more intently than on the few previous occasions, he looked across the road.

Again a few trucks just rumbled past.

But in an instant it all went still. When he caught sight of him. The man in grayish-brown. And there was no doubt. As if lazily, nonchalantly absorbed in the sidewalk in front of him, he was walking there on the other side. Parallel, one might say . . . This couldn't be a coincidence. Valent, confused by the again-searing pain in his heart, made himself think about the towers, the concrete slope, and also about the not-so-very-distant intersection in the haze ahead. What seemed best to him, in fact, was to just keep walking along as if free of cares, while maintaining the demeanor and light-hearted step of a man out on a stroll with as much dignity as possible . . . and then, there at the intersection, maybe find a chance to duck out of sight, to dash off down one of the nearest streets and get away. Maybe he'd even be able to catch a cab. Or the streetcar could arrive at exactly the right time. Either of these things or, who knows, some third thing, might unexpectedly come to his rescue; and at the same time, it would be indisputable proof that turning back toward the towers was not the right choice.

The fat man must have had him in his sights all this time. But still, he nursed a quiet hope that maybe, at the last moment (as is sometimes accompanied by a bass tremolo), an opportunity would present itself and rescue him, and this hope spurred him on and gave him courage. Written on the concrete slope, in black and edged in silver, was the word ULTRAS . . . "Keep going, keep walking," he told himself over and over, "just like this, just strolling along . . ." And he tried to breathe away the tightness, the stiffness in his legs, and tried to assess things, what to do and how to do it, about the traffic light, and the lines of waiting vehicles . . .

The word MARINA was written there, on the corner, in front of the traffic light; a few pedestrians were waiting to cross. He did not care to look across the road. He simply turned right, and started down the street . . . and immediately turned back and, furtively hugging the wall, made his way among the other crisscrossing pedestrians to the passageway beneath the main road, past a group of beggars, and again up the first set of steps . . . where, before stepping onto the sidewalk in the open air, he nonetheless looked this way and the other but didn't see anyone who looked suspicious . . . True, quite a few people turned and looked at him when he was skulking along like that, when he was being so wary. But they just went on their way. He, too, now went on his way and very soon turned again, but, as if on purpose, there were no streetcars coming, and no taxicabs; but there were these short, narrow, densely tangled streets that enabled him to keep changing direction, to stop at one corner or another, catch his breath, look all around, and—despite his heart, despite this suspiciously clenching pain, despite everything—to hurry on, through colorfully, sometimes garishly, dressed people who moved out of his way, who bumped into him (one did say "pardon me"); to hurry to one then the other side of the street, through an arcade, past some sort of government offices, past the "Jereb" law office . . . and who knows how many streets away to find himself heading again toward the noise of traffic and emergency sirens . . . but the noise was receding somehow, getting lost, sinking, as it were, behind the ever more densely, ever more unfathomably sprawling, interlacing lines of façades and colonnades and arcades and streets, again and again, streets that didn't take him there, to the noise, to the streetcars and taxicabs . . . A few of these streets ended at concrete barriers, in places overgrown with vegetation. And down below, in the deep walled ravine beneath the barrier, there was stillness, a sparkling brightness that seemed to beckon playfully, a pleasant coolness, a pleasant peace . . .

He was, in fact, not surprised when he again saw, across the street, the fat man. Looking worn out. Too fat. In an unbuttoned, black-lined jacket. He might even give the man a little smile from across the street. Since now it wasn't about escape. "Keep going. Hah . . ." As long as you can. From some windows nearby came the sound of old women's voices singing very slowly. And then it died away. Behind a corner. The streets were getting narrower. The fat man was wheezing. And was falling behind a little, too. Vestibules and cellars emitted the smell of decay onto the street. Peace could be felt in the breeze that came from the river in the ravine. And there would be no sense in running from that peace . . . Hurrying, he removed his jacket without stopping and tossed it back toward the fat man. He took off his ring too, and his necktie, ripped off his shirt, and flung them all away . . .

Then he stopped.

And waited.

The fat man, pale and wheezing heavily, also stopped.

"Look, Pavlovski!" He smiled at that unhealthy-looking, florid face. "The ones who know how to do it . . . they can fly." You just spread your arms out like this, into the silence.

In 2010, the Slovenian Book Agency took a bold step toward solving the problem of how few literary works are now translated into English, initiating a program to provide financial support for a series dedicated to Slovenian literature at Dalkey Archive Press. Partially evolving from a relationship that Dalkey Archive and the Vilenica International Literary Festival had developed a few years previously, this new program begins with the publication of three Slovenian novels in its first year, and will go on to ensure that both classic and contemporary works from Slovenian are brought into English, while allowing the Press to undertake marketing efforts far exceeding what publishers can normally provide for works in translation.

Slovenia has always held a great reverence for literature, with the Slovenian national identity being forged through its fiction and poetry long before the foundation of the contemporary Republic: "It is precisely literature that has in some profound, subtle sense safeguarded the Slovenian community from the imperialistic appetites of stronger and more expansive nations in the region," writes critic Andrej Inkret. Never insular, Slovenian writing has long been in dialogue with the great movements of world literature, from the romantic to the experimental, seeing the literary not as distinct from the world, but as an integral means of perceiving and even amending it.

VLADO ŽABOT is the author of several novels, and has been the recipient of both the prestigious Prešeren Fund Award and the Kresnik Prize for Best Novel of the Year. Since 2003, he has been the president of the Slovene Writers' Association.

RAWLEY GRAU's translations include *The Hidden Handshake*, a collection of essays by Ales Debeljak, and *Family Parables*, a book of short fiction by Boris Pintar. NIKOLAI JEFFS teaches cultural theory at the Faculty of Arts, University of Ljubljana.

MAX FRISCH, *I'm Not Stiller.*
Man in the Holocene.
CARLOS FUENTES, *Christopher Unborn.*
Distant Relations.
Terra Nostra.
Where the Air Is Clear.
JANICE GALLOWAY, *Foreign Parts.*
The Trick Is to Keep Breathing.
WILLIAM H. GASS, *Cartesian Sonata*
and Other Novellas.
Finding a Form.
A Temple of Texts.
The Tunnel.
Willie Masters' Lonesome Wife.
GÉRARD GAVARRY, *Hoppla! 1 2 3.*
ETIENNE GILSON,
The Arts of the Beautiful.
Forms and Substances in the Arts.
C. S. GISCOMBE, *Giscome Road.*
Here.
Prairie Style.
DOUGLAS GLOVER, *Bad News of the Heart.*
The Enamoured Knight.
WITOLD GOMBROWICZ,
A Kind of Testament.
KAREN ELIZABETH GORDON,
The Red Shoes.
GEORGI GOSPODINOV, *Natural Novel.*
JUAN GOYTISOLO, *Count Julian.*
Juan the Landless.
Makbara.
Marks of Identity.
PATRICK GRAINVILLE, *The Cave of Heaven.*
HENRY GREEN, *Back.*
Blindness.
Concluding.
Doting.
Nothing.
JIŘÍ GRUŠA, *The Questionnaire.*
GABRIEL GUDDING,
Rhode Island Notebook.
MELA HARTWIG, *Am I a Redundant*
Human Being?
JOHN HAWKES, *The Passion Artist.*
Whistlejacket.
ALEKSANDAR HEMON, ED.,
Best European Fiction.
AIDAN HIGGINS, *A Bestiary.*
Balcony of Europe.
Bornholm Night-Ferry.
Darkling Plain: Texts for the Air.
Flotsam and Jetsam.
Langrishe, Go Down.
Scenes from a Receding Past.
Windy Arbours.
KEIZO HINO, *Isle of Dreams.*
ALDOUS HUXLEY, *Antic Hay.*
Crome Yellow.
Point Counter Point.
Those Barren Leaves.
Time Must Have a Stop.
MIKHAIL IOSSEL AND JEFF PARKER, EDS.,
Amerika: Russian Writers View the
United States.
GERT JONKE, *The Distant Sound.*
Geometric Regional Novel.

Homage to Czerny.
The System of Vienna.
JACQUES JOUET, *Mountain R.*
Savage.
CHARLES JULIET, *Conversations with*
Samuel Beckett and Bram van
Velde.
MIEKO KANAI, *The Word Book.*
YORAM KANIUK, *Life on Sandpaper.*
HUGH KENNER, *The Counterfeiters.*
Flaubert, Joyce and Beckett:
The Stoic Comedians.
Joyce's Voices.
DANILO KIŠ, *Garden, Ashes.*
A Tomb for Boris Davidovich.
ANITA KONKKA, *A Fool's Paradise.*
GEORGE KONRÁD, *The City Builder.*
TADEUSZ KONWICKI, *A Minor Apocalypse.*
The Polish Complex.
MENIS KOUMANDAREAS, *Koula.*
ELAINE KRAF, *The Princess of 72nd Street.*
JIM KRUSOE, *Iceland.*
EWA KURYLUK, *Century 21.*
EMILIO LASCANO TEGUI, *On Elegance*
While Sleeping.
ERIC LAURRENT, *Do Not Touch.*
VIOLETTE LEDUC, *La Bâtarde.*
SUZANNE JILL LEVINE, *The Subversive*
Scribe: Translating Latin
American Fiction.
DEBORAH LEVY, *Billy and Girl.*
Pillow Talk in Europe and Other
Places.
JOSÉ LEZAMA LIMA, *Paradiso.*
ROSA LIKSOM, *Dark Paradise.*
OSMAN LINS, *Avalovara.*
The Queen of the Prisons of Greece.
ALF MAC LOCHLAINN,
The Corpus in the Library.
Out of Focus.
RON LOEWINSOHN, *Magnetic Field(s).*
BRIAN LYNCH, *The Winner of Sorrow.*
D. KEITH MANO, *Take Five.*
MICHELINE AHARONIAN MARCOM,
The Mirror in the Well.
BEN MARCUS,
The Age of Wire and String.
WALLACE MARKFIELD,
Teitlebaum's Window.
To an Early Grave.
DAVID MARKSON, *Reader's Block.*
Springer's Progress.
Wittgenstein's Mistress.
CAROLE MASO, *AVA.*
LADISLAV MATEJKA AND KRYSTYNA
POMORSKA, EDS.,
Readings in Russian Poetics:
Formalist and Structuralist Views.
HARRY MATHEWS,
The Case of the Persevering Maltese:
Collected Essays.
Cigarettes.
The Conversions.
The Human Country: New and
Collected Stories.
The Journalist.

SELECTED DALKEY ARCHIVE PAPERBACKS

My Life in CIA.
Singular Pleasures.
The Sinking of the Odradek
   Stadium.
Tlooth.
20 Lines a Day.
JOSEPH MCELROY,
   Night Soul and Other Stories.
ROBERT L. MCLAUGHLIN, ED.,
   Innovations: An Anthology of
   Modern & Contemporary Fiction.
HERMAN MELVILLE, *The Confidence-Man.*
AMANDA MICHALOPOULOU, *I'd Like.*
STEVEN MILLHAUSER,
   The Barnum Museum.
   In the Penny Arcade.
RALPH J. MILLS, JR.,
   Essays on Poetry.
MOMUS, *The Book of Jokes.*
CHRISTINE MONTALBETTI, *Western.*
OLIVE MOORE, *Spleen.*
NICHOLAS MOSLEY, *Accident.*
   Assassins.
   Catastrophe Practice.
   Children of Darkness and Light.
   Experience and Religion.
   God's Hazard.
   The Hesperides Tree.
   Hopeful Monsters.
   Imago Bird.
   Impossible Object.
   Inventing God.
   Judith.
   Look at the Dark.
   Natalie Natalia.
   Paradoxes of Peace.
   Serpent.
   Time at War.
   The Uses of Slime Mould:
   Essays of Four Decades.
WARREN MOTTE,
   Fables of the Novel: French Fiction
   since 1990.
   Fiction Now: The French Novel in
   the 21st Century.
   Oulipo: A Primer of Potential
   Literature.
YVES NAVARRE, *Our Share of Time.*
   Sweet Tooth.
DOROTHY NELSON, *In Night's City.*
   Tar and Feathers.
ESHKOL NEVO, *Homesick.*
WILFRIDO D. NOLLEDO,
   But for the Lovers.
FLANN O'BRIEN,
   At Swim-Two-Birds.
   At War.
   The Best of Myles.
   The Dalkey Archive.
   Further Cuttings.
   The Hard Life.
   The Poor Mouth.
   The Third Policeman.
CLAUDE OLLIER, *The Mise-en-Scène.*
PATRIK OUŘEDNÍK, *Europeana.*
BORIS PAHOR, *Necropolis.*

FERNANDO DEL PASO,
   News from the Empire.
   Palinuro of Mexico.
ROBERT PINGET, *The Inquisitory.*
   Mahu or The Material.
   Trio.
MANUEL PUIG,
   Betrayed by Rita Hayworth.
   The Buenos Aires Affair.
   Heartbreak Tango.
RAYMOND QUENEAU, *The Last Days.*
   Odile.
   Pierrot Mon Ami.
   Saint Glinglin.
ANN QUIN, *Berg.*
   Passages.
   Three.
   Tripticks.
ISHMAEL REED,
   The Free-Lance Pallbearers.
   The Last Days of Louisiana Red.
   Ishmael Reed: The Plays.
   Reckless Eyeballing.
   The Terrible Threes.
   The Terrible Twos.
   Yellow Back Radio Broke-Down.
JEAN RICARDOU, *Place Names.*
RAINER MARIA RILKE, *The Notebooks of*
   Malte Laurids Brigge.
JULIÁN RÍOS, *The House of Ulysses.*
   Larva: A Midsummer Night's Babel.
   Poundemonium.
AUGUSTO ROA BASTOS, *I the Supreme.*
DANIËL ROBBERECHTS,
   Arriving in Avignon.
OLIVIER ROLIN, *Hotel Crystal.*
ALIX CLEO ROUBAUD, *Alix's Journal.*
JACQUES ROUBAUD, *The Form of a*
   City Changes Faster, Alas, Than
   the Human Heart.
   The Great Fire of London.
   Hortense in Exile.
   Hortense Is Abducted.
   The Loop.
   The Plurality of Worlds of Lewis.
   The Princess Hoppy.
   Some Thing Black.
LEON S. ROUDIEZ,
   French Fiction Revisited.
VEDRANA RUDAN, *Night.*
STIG SÆTERBAKKEN, *Siamese.*
LYDIE SALVAYRE, *The Company of Ghosts.*
   Everyday Life.
   The Lecture.
   Portrait of the Writer as a
   Domesticated Animal.
   The Power of Flies.
LUIS RAFAEL SÁNCHEZ,
   Macho Camacho's Beat.
SEVERO SARDUY, *Cobra & Maitreya.*
NATHALIE SARRAUTE,
   Do You Hear Them?
   Martereau.
   The Planetarium.
ARNO SCHMIDT, *Collected Stories.*
   Nobodaddy's Children.

SELECTED DALKEY ARCHIVE PAPERBACKS

CHRISTINE SCHUTT, *Nightwork.*
GAIL SCOTT, *My Paris.*
DAMION SEARLS, *What We Were Doing
and Where We Were Going.*
JUNE AKERS SEESE,
Is This What Other Women Feel Too?
What Waiting Really Means.
BERNARD SHARE, *Inish.*
Transit.
AURELIE SHEEHAN,
Jack Kerouac Is Pregnant.
VIKTOR SHKLOVSKY, *Knight's Move.*
*A Sentimental Journey:
Memoirs 1917–1922.*
Energy of Delusion: A Book on Plot.
Literature and Cinematography.
Theory of Prose.
Third Factory.
Zoo, or Letters Not about Love.
CLAUDE SIMON, *The Invitation.*
PIERRE SINIAC, *The Collaborators.*
JOSEF ŠKVORECKÝ, *The Engineer of
Human Souls.*
GILBERT SORRENTINO,
Aberration of Starlight.
Blue Pastoral.
Crystal Vision.
*Imaginative Qualities of Actual
Things.*
Mulligan Stew.
Pack of Lies.
Red the Fiend.
The Sky Changes.
Something Said.
Splendide-Hôtel.
Steelwork.
Under the Shadow.
W. M. SPACKMAN,
The Complete Fiction.
ANDRZEJ STASIUK, *Fado.*
GERTRUDE STEIN,
Lucy Church Amiably.
The Making of Americans.
A Novel of Thank You.
LARS SVENDSEN, *A Philosophy of Evil.*
PIOTR SZEWC, *Annihilation.*
GONÇALO M. TAVARES, *Jerusalem.*
LUCIAN DAN TEODOROVICI,
Our Circus Presents . . .
STEFAN THEMERSON, *Hobson's Island.*
The Mystery of the Sardine.
Tom Harris.
JOHN TOOMEY, *Sleepwalker.*
JEAN-PHILIPPE TOUSSAINT,
The Bathroom.
Camera.
Monsieur.
Running Away.
Self-Portrait Abroad.
Television.
DUMITRU TSEPENEAG,
Hotel Europa.
The Necessary Marriage.
Pigeon Post.
Vain Art of the Fugue.
ESTHER TUSQUETS, *Stranded.*

DUBRAVKA UGRESIC,
Lend Me Your Character.
Thank You for Not Reading.
MATI UNT, *Brecht at Night.*
Diary of a Blood Donor.
Things in the Night.
ÁLVARO URIBE AND OLIVIA SEARS, EDS.,
*Best of Contemporary Mexican
Fiction.*
ELOY URROZ, *Friction.*
The Obstacles.
LUISA VALENZUELA, *He Who Searches.*
MARJA-LIISA VARTIO,
The Parson's Widow.
PAUL VERHAEGHEN, *Omega Minor.*
BORIS VIAN, *Heartsnatcher.*
LLORENÇ VILLALONGA, *The Dolls' Room.*
ORNELA VORPSI, *The Country Where No
One Ever Dies.*
AUSTRYN WAINHOUSE, *Hedyphagetica.*
PAUL WEST,
Words for a Deaf Daughter & Gala.
CURTIS WHITE,
America's Magic Mountain.
The Idea of Home.
Memories of My Father Watching TV.
*Monstrous Possibility: An Invitation
to Literary Politics.*
Requiem.
DIANE WILLIAMS, *Excitability:
Selected Stories.*
Romancer Erector.
DOUGLAS WOOLF, *Wall to Wall.*
Ya! & John-Juan.
JAY WRIGHT, *Polynomials and Pollen.*
*The Presentable Art of Reading
Absence.*
PHILIP WYLIE, *Generation of Vipers.*
MARGUERITE YOUNG,
Angel in the Forest.
Miss MacIntosh, My Darling.
REYOUNG, *Unbabbling.*
VLADO ŽABOT, *The Succubus.*
ZORAN ŽIVKOVIĆ, *Hidden Camera.*
LOUIS ZUKOFSKY, *Collected Fiction.*
SCOTT ZWIREN, *God Head.*

FOR A FULL LIST OF PUBLICATIONS, VISIT:
www.dalkeyarchive.com